Philip Doddridge

Some remarkable passages in the life of the Hon. Col. James Gardiner

1745

Philip Doddridge

Some remarkable passages in the life of the Hon. Col. James Gardiner
1745

ISBN/EAN: 9783337196523

Printed in Europe, USA, Canada, Australia, Japan

Cover: Foto ©Raphael Reischuk / pixelio.de

More available books at **www.hansebooks.com**

SOME

REMARKABLE P▮▮▮▮▮

IN THE

LIFE

OF THE

Hon. Col. JAMES GARDINER,

WHO WAS SLAIN AT THE

BATTLE of PRESTON PANS,

SEPTEMBER 21, 1745.

TO WHICH IS ADDED,

The SERMON,

OCCASIONED BY HIS

HEROICK DEATH.

BY P. DODDRIDGE, D. D.

———————Juftior alter
Nec Pietate fuit, nec Bello major & Armis. Virg.

PRINTED AT *BOSTON*,
BY I. THOMAS AND E. T. ANDREWS,
FAUST's STATUE, No. 45, *Newbury Street.*

M,DCC,XCII.

David Gardiner, Esq.

CORNET in SIR JOHN COPE's

REGIMENT of DRAGOONS.

DEAR SIR,

WHILE my heart is following you with a truly paternal folicitude, through all the dangers of military life, in which you are thus early engaged, anxious for your fafety amidft the inftruments of death, and the far more dangerous allurements of vice; I feel a peculiar pleaſure in being able at length, though after fuch long delays, to put into your hands the Memoirs with which I now prefent you. They contain many particulars, which would have been worthy of your attentive notice, had they related to a perfon of the moft diftant nation or age: But they will, I doubt not, command your peculiar regard, as they are facred to the memory of that excellent man, from whom you had the honour to derive your birth, and by whofe generous and affectionate care you have been laid under all the obligations which the beft of fathers could confer on a

HERE

Here, Sir, you fee a gentleman, who with all the advantages of a liberal and religious education, added to every natural accomplishment that could render him most agreeable, entered, before he had attained the stature of a man, on those arduous and generous services to which you are devoted, and behaved in them with a gallantry and courage, which will always give a splendor to his name among the British soldiery, and render him an example to all officers of his rank. But alas! amidst all the intrepidity of the martial Hero, you see him vanquished by the blandishments of pleasure, and in chace of it plunging himself into follies and vices, for which no want of education or genius could have been a sufficient excuse. You behold him urging the ignoble and fatal pursuit, unmoved by the terrors which death was continually darting around him, and the most signal deliverances by which Providence again and again rescued him from those terrors; till at length he was reclaimed by an ever memorable interposition of divine grace. Then you have the pleasure of seeing him become in good earnest *a Convert to Christianity*, and by speedy advances growing up into one of its brightest ornaments; his mind continually filled with the great ideas which the gospel of our Redeemer suggests, and bringing the blessed influence of its sublime principles into every relation

of

of military and civil, of public and domeſtic life.
You trace him perſevering in a ſteady and uni-
form courſe of goodneſs, through a long ſeries
of honourable and proſperous years, the delight of all that were ſo happy as to know him,
and, in his ſphere, the moſt faithful guardian of his country; till at laſt, worn out with
honourable labours, and broken with infirmities
which they had haſtened upon him before the
time, you ſee him forgetting them at once at the
call of duty and Providence; with all the generous ardour of his moſt vigorous days ruſhing
on the enemies of religion and liberty, ſuſtaining
their ſhock with the moſt deliberate fortitude,
when deſerted by thoſe that ſhould have ſupported him, and cheerfully ſacrificing the little
remains of a mortal life, in the triumphant views
of a glorious immortality.

This, Sir, is the noble object I preſent to
your view; and you will, I hope, fix your eye
continually upon it; and will never allow yourſelf for one day to forget, that this illuſtrious
man is COLONEL GARDINER, your ever honoured father; who having approved his *fidelity
to the death* and received a *crown of life*, ſeems as
it were, by what you here read, to be calling out
to you from amidſt the cloud of witneſſes with
which you are ſurrounded, and urging you by
                                        every

every generous, tender, filial sentiment, to mark the footsteps of his Christian race, and strenuously to maintain that combat, where the victory is through divine grace certain, and the prize an eternal kingdom in the Heavens.

My hopes, Sir, that all these powerful motives will especially have their full efficacy on you, are greatly encouraged by the certainty which I have of your being well acquainted with the evidence of Christianity in its full extent; a criminal ignorance of which, in the midst of great advantages for learning them, leaves so many of our young people a prey to Deism, and so to vice and ruin, which generally bring up its rear. My life would be a continual burthen to me, if I had not a consciousness in the sight of God, that during the years in which the important trust of your education was committed to my care, I had laid before you the proofs both of natural and revealed religion, in what I assuredly esteem to be, with regard to the judgment, if they are carefully examined, an irresistable light; and that I had endeavoured to attend them with those addresses, which might be most likely to impress your heart. You have not, dear Sir, forgotten, and I am confident you can never entirely forget, the assiduity with which I have laboured to form your mind, not only to what

might

might be ornamental to you in human life, but above all, to a true taste of what is really excellent, and an early contempt of thofe vanities by which the generality of our youth, efpecially in your ftation, are debafed, enervated, and undone. My private, as well as publick addreffes for this purpofe will, I know, be remembered by you, and the tears of tendernefs with which they have fo often been accompanied : And may they be fo remembered, that they who are moft tenderly concerned, may be comforted under the lofs of fuch an ineftimable friend as COLONEL GARDI-NER, by feeing that his character, in all its moft amiable and refplendent parts, lives in you ; and that how difficult foever it may be to act up to that height of expectation, with which the eyes of the world will be fixed on the fon of fuch a father, you are, in the ftrength of divine grace, attempting it ; at leaft are following him with generous emulation, and with daily folicitude, that the fteps may be lefs unequal !

May the Lord God of your Father, and I will add, of both your pious and honourable parents, animate your heart more and more with fuch views and fentiments as thefe ! May he guard your life amidft every fcene of danger, to be a protection and bleffing to thofe that are yet unborn; and may he give you, in fome far diftant

period

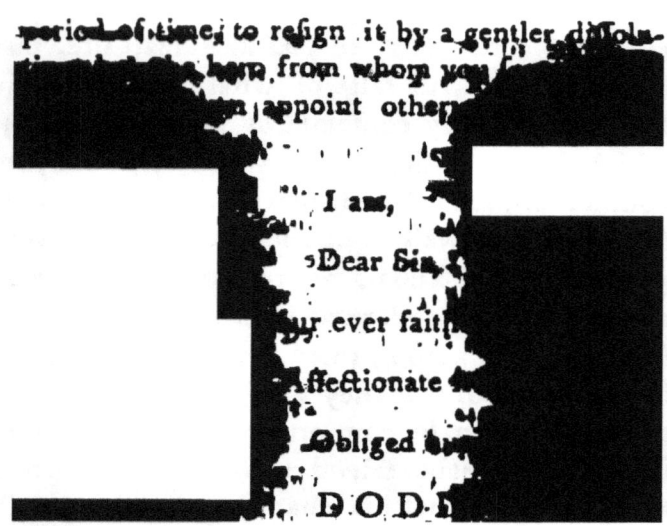

DEDICATION.

period of time, to refign it by a gentler diffolu-
tion ..... the hand from whom you .....
..... appoint other .....

I am,

Dear Sir,

.....ur ever faith.....

.....ffectionate .....

.....bliged .....

D. O. D. .....

L I F E

OF THE

Hon. Col. JAMES GARDINER.

WHEN I promifed the public fome larger account of the life and char-acter of this illuftrious perfon, than I could conveniently infert in my fermon on the fad occafion of his death, I was fecure, that if Providence continued my capacity of writing, I fhould not wholly difappoint the expectation. For I was furnifhed with a variety of particulars, which appeared to me worthy of general notice, in confequence of that intimate friendfhip with which he had honored me during the fix laft years of his life ; a friendfhip which led him to open

B his

his heart to me in repeated converſations, with an unbounded confidence, (as he then aſſured me, beyond what he had uſed with any other man living) ſo far as religious experiences were concerned : And I had alſo received ſeveral very valuable letters from him, during the time of our abſence from each other, which contained moſt genuine and edifying traces of his Chriſtian character. But I hoped farther to learn many valuable particulars from the papers of his own cloſet ; and from his letters to other friends, as well as from what they more circumſtantially knew concerning him : I therefore determined to delay the execution of my promiſe, till I could enjoy theſe advantages for performing it in the moſt ſatisfactory manner ; nor have I, on the whole, reaſon to regret that determination.

I ſhall not trouble the reader with all the cauſes which concurred to hinder theſe expected aſſiſtances for almoſt a whole year : the chief of them were the tedious languiſhing illneſs of his afflicted lady, through whoſe hands it was proper the papers ſhould paſs ; together with the confuſion into which the rebels had thrown them, when they ranſacked his ſeat at Bankton, where moſt of them were depoſited. But having now received

ſuch

fuch of them as have efcaped their voracious hands, and could conveniently be collected and tranfmitted, I fet myfelf with the greateft pleafure to perform, what I efteem, not merely a tribute of gratitude to the memory of my invaluable friend, (though never was the memory of any mortal man more precious and facred to me) but of duty to God, and to my fellow creatures : for I have a moft cheerful hope, that the narrative I am now to write, will, under the divine blefling, be a means of fpreading, what of all things in the world every benevolent heart will moft defire to fpread, a warm and lively fenfe of religion.

My own heart has been fo much edified and animated, by what I have read in the memoirs of perfons who have been eminent for wifdom and piety, that I cannot but wifh the treafure may be more and more increafed : and I would hope, the world may gather the like valuable fruits from the Life I am now attempting ; not only as it will contain very fingular circumftances, which may excite a general curiofity, but as it comes attended with fome other particular advantages.

The reader is here to furvey a character of fuch eminent and various goodnefs, as
                                        might

might demand veneration, and infpire him with a defire to imitate it too, had it appeared in the obfcureft rank : but it will furely command fome particular regard, when viewed in fo elevated and important a ftation ; efpecially as it fhone, not in ecclefiaftical, but military life, where the temptations are fo many, and the prevalency of the contrary chara&er fo great, that it may feem no inconfiderable praife and felicity to be free from diffolute vice, and to retain what in moft other profeffions might be efteemed only a *mediocrity of virtue*. It may furely with the higheft juftice be expe&ed, that the title and bravery of Colonel *Gardiner* will invite many of our officers and foldiers, to whom his name has been long honorable and dear, to perufe this account of him with fome peculiar attention : in confequence of which, it may be a means of increafing the number, and brightening the chara&er, of thofe who are already adorning their office, their country, and their religion ; and of reclaiming thofe, who will fee rather what they ought to be, than what they are. On the whole, to the *gentlemen of the fword* I would particularly offer thefe memoirs, as theirs by fo diftinguifhed a title : yet I am firmly perfuaded there are none whofe office is fo

                                        facred

facred, or whofe proficiency in the religious life is fo advanced, but they may find fomething to demand their thankfulnefs, and to awaken their emulation.

Col. James Gardiner, of whom we write, was the fon of Capt. Patrick Gardiner, of the family of Torwood-head, by Mrs. Mary Hodge, of the family of Gladfmuir. The Captain, who was mafter of a handfome eftate, ferved many years in the army of King William and Queen Anne, and died abroad with the Britifh forces in Germany, quickly after the battle of Hochftet, through the fatigues he underwent in the duties of that celebrated campaign. He had a company in the regiment of foot, once commanded by Colonel Hodge, his valiant brother in law, who was flain at the head of that regiment, my memorial from Scotland fays, at the battle of Steenkirk, which was faught in the year 1692.

Mrs. Gardiner, our Colonel's mother, was a lady of a very valuable character ; but it pleafed God to exercife her with very uncommon trials : for fhe not only loft her hufband and her brother in the fervice of their country, as before related, but alfo her eldeft fon, Mr. Robert Gardiner, on the day which completed the fixteenth year of his

age,

age, at the fiege of Namur, in 1695. But there is reafon to believe, God bleffed thefe various and heavy afflictions, as the means of forming her to that eminent degree of piety, which will render her memory honorable as long as it continues.

Her fecond fon, the worthy perfon of whom I am now to give a more particular account, was born at Carriden in Linlithgowfhire, on the 10th of January, A. D. 1687-8, the memorable year of that glorious Revolution, which he juftly efteemed among the happieft of all events. So that when he was flain in the defence of thofe liberties, which God then by fo gracious a providence refcued from utter deftruction, *i. e.* on the 21ft of September, 1745, he was aged 57 years, 8 months, and 11 days.

The annual return of his birth day was obferved by him, in the latter and better years of his life, in a manner very different from what is commonly practifed : For inftead of making it a day of feftivity, I am told, he rather diftinguifhed it as a feafon of more than ordinary humiliation before God; both in commemoration of thofe mercies which he received in the firft opening of life, and under an affectionate fenfe, as well of his long alienation from the Great Author

thor

thor and fupport of his being, as of the many imperfections which he lamented, in the beft of his days and fervices.

I have not met with many things remarkable concerning the early years of his life, only that his mother took care to inftruct him, with great tendernefs and affection, in the principles of true chriftianity. He was alfo trained up in human literature at the fchool at Linlithgow, where he made a very confiderable progrefs in the languages. I remember to have heard him quote fome paffages of the Latin claffics very pertinently; though his employment in life, and the various turns which his mind took under different impulfes in fucceeding years, prevented him from cultivating fuch ftudies.

The good effects of his mother's prudent and exemplary care were not fo confpicuous as fhe wifhed and hoped, in the younger part of her fon's life; yet there is great reafon to believe, they were not entirely loft. As they were probably the occafion of many convictions, which in his younger years were overborne; fo I doubt not, that when religious impreffions took that ftrong hold of his heart, which they afterwards did, that ftock of knowledge which had been fo early laid up in his mind, was found of confider-

able

able fervice. And I have heard them make the obfervation, as an encouragement to parents, and other pious friends, to do their duty, and to hope for thofe good confequences of it which may not immediately appear.

Could his mother, or a very religious aunt (of whofe good inftructions and exhortations I have often heard him fpeak with pleafure) have prevailed, he would not have thought of a *military life ;* from which, it is no wonder, thefe ladies endeavoured to diffuade him, confidering the mournful experience they had of the dangers attending it, and the dear relatives they had loft already by it. But it fuited his tafte ; and the ardour of his fpirit, animated by the perfuafions of a friend who greatly urged it,* was not to be reftrained. Nor will the reader wonder, that thus excited and fupported, it eafily overbore their tender remonftrances, when he knows, that this lively youth faught *three duels* before he attained to the ftature of a man ; in one of which, when he was but eight years old, he received from a boy much older than himfelf, a wound in his right cheek, the fcar of which was always very apparent.

* I fuppofe this to have been General Rue, who had from his childhood a peculiar affection for him.

parent.   The falfe fenfe of honor which in-
ftigated him to it, might feem indeed fomething excufeable, in thofe unripened years,
and confidering the profeffion of his father,
brother, and uncle ; but I have often heard
him mention this rafhnefs with that regret
which the reflection would naturally give to
fo wife and good a man in the maturity of
life.   And I have been informed, that after
his remarkable converfion, he declined accepting a challenge, with this calm and truly
great reply, which in a man of his experienced bravery was exceeding graceful : " I
fear finning, though you know I do not fear
fighting."

He ferved firft as a Cadet, which muft
have been very early ; and then, at 14 years
old, he bore an Enfign's commiffion in a
Scots regiment in the Dutch fervice ; in
which he continued till the year 1702, when
(if my information be right) he received an
Enfign's commiffion from Queen Anne,
which he bore in the battle of Ramillies,
being then in the 19th year of his age.   In
this ever memorable action, he received a
wound in his mouth by a mufket ball, which
hath often been reported to be the occafion
of his converfion.   That report was a miftaken one ; but as fome very remarkable
circumftances

circumſtances attended this affair, which I have had the pleaſure of hearing more than once from his own mouth, I hope my reader will excuſe me, if I give him ſo uncommon a ſtory at large.

Our young officer was of a party in the Forlorn Hope, and was commanded on what ſeemed almoſt a deſperate ſervice, to diſpoſſeſs the French of the church yard at Ramillies, where a conſiderable number of them were poſted to remarkable advantage. They ſucceeded much better than was expected ; and it may be well ſuppoſed, that Mr. Gardiner, who had before been in ſeveral encounters, and had the view of making his fortune, to animate the natural intrepidity of his ſpirit, was glad of ſuch an opportunity of ſignalizing himſelf. Accordingly he had planted his colours on an advanced ground ; and while he was calling to his men, (probably in that horrid language which is ſo peculiar a diſgrace to our ſoldiery, and ſo abſurdly common in ſuch articles of extreme danger) he received a ſhot into his mouth ; which, without beating out any of his teeth, or touching the fore part of his tongue, went through his neck, and came out about an inch and an half on the left ſide of the *vertebræ*. Not

feeling

feeling, at firſt, the pain of the ſtroke, he wondered what was become of the ball, and in the wildneſs of his ſurprize, began to ſuſ-pect he had ſwallowed it ; but dropping ſoon after, he traced the paſſage of it by his finger, when he could diſcover it no other way ; which I mention as one circumſtance among many which occur, to make it pro-bable that the greater part of thoſe who fall in battle by theſe inſtruments of death, feel very little anguiſh from the moſt mortal wounds.

This accident happened about five or ſix in the evening, on the 23d day of May, in the year 1706 ; and the army purſuing its advantages againſt the French, without ever regarding the wounded, (which was, it ſeems, the Duke of Marlborough's conſtant method) our young officer lay all night in the field, agitated, as well may be ſuppoſed, with a great variety of thoughts.   He aſſur-ed me, that when he reflected upon the cir-cumſtances of his wound, that a ball ſhould, as he then conceived it, go through his head without killing him, he thought God had preſerved him by miracle ; and therefore aſſuredly concluded that he ſhould live, abandoned and deſperate as his ſtate then ſeemed to be.   Yet, which to me appeared

very

very aftonifhing he had little thoughts of humbling himfelf before God, and return-.ing to him after the wanderings of a life fo licentioufly begun. But expecting to re-.cover, his mind was taken up with contriv-ances to fecure his gold, of which he had a pretty deal about him ; and he had recourfe to a very odd expedient, which proved fuc-cefsful. Expecting to be ftripped, he firft took out a handful of that clotted gore, of which he was freequently obliged to clear his mouth, or he would have been choaked ; and putting it into his left hand, he took out his money, (which I think, was about 19 piftoles) and fhutting his hand, and bef-mearing the back part of it with blood, he kept it in this pofition till the blood dried in fuch a manner that his hand could not eafily fall open, though any fudden furprize fhould happen, in which he might lofe the prefence of mind which that conceal-ment otherwife would have required.

In the morning the French, who were mafters of that fpot, though their forces were defeated at fome diftance, came to plunder the flain ; and feeing him to ap-pearance almoft expiring, one of them was juft applying a fword to his breaft, to def-troy the little remainder of life ; when in the

the critical moment, upon which all the extraordinary events of such a life as his afterwards proved were suspended, a cordelier, who attended the plunderers, interposed, taking him by his dress for a Frenchman; and said, " Do not kill that poor child." Our young soldier heard all that passed, though he was not able to speak one word; and opening his eyes, made a sign for something to drink. They gave him a sup of some spirituous liquor, which happened to be at hand; by which he said he found a more sensible refreshment, than he could remember from any thing he had tasted either before or since. Then signing to the Friar to lean down his ear to his mouth, he employed the first efforts of his feeble breath in telling him, (what, alas! was a contrived falsehood) that he was nephew to the Governor of Huy, a neutral town in the neighborhood, and that, if he could take any method of conveying him thither, he did not doubt but his uncle would liberally reward him. He had indeed a friend at Huy, (who I think was Governor, and if I mistake not, had been acquainted with the Captain his father) from whom he expected a kind reception; but the relation was only pretended. On hearing this, they laid him on a sort of hand barrow, and sent

him by a file of mufqueteers towards the
place ; but the men loft their way, and got
into a wood towards the evening, 'in which
they were obliged to continue all night.
The poor patient's wound being ftill un-
dreffed, it is not to be wondered that by
this time it raged violently.   The anguifh
of it engaged him earneftly to beg, that they
would either kill him outright, or leave him
there to die, without the torture of any farther motion ; and indeed they were obliged
to reft for a confiderable time, on account
of their own wearinefs.   Thus he fpent the
fecond night in the open air, without any
thing more than a common bandage to
ftanch the blood.   He hath often mentioned it as a moft aftonifhing providence, that
he did not bleed to death ; which, under
God, he afcribed to the remarkable coldnefs
of thefe two nights.

Judging it quite unfafe to attempt carry-
ing him to Huy, from whence they were
now feveral miles diftant, his convoy took
him early in the morning to a convent in.
the neighborhood ; where he was hofpitably
received, and treated with great kindnefs and
tendernefs.   But the cure of his wound was
committed to an ignorant barber furgeon,
who lived near the houfe ; the beft fhift that
could then be made, at a time when it may
eafily

eafily be fuppofed perfons of ability in their profeffion had their hands full of employment.   The tent which this artift applied, was almoft like a peg driven into the wound; and gentlemen of fkill and experience, when they came to hear of the manner in which he was treated, wondered how he could poffibly furvive fuch management.   But by the bleffing of God on thefe applications, rough as they were, he recovered in a few months.   The Lady Abbefs, who called him her fon, treated him with the affection and care of a mother; and he always declared, that every thing which he faw within thefe walls, was conducted with the ftricteft decency and decorum.   He received a great many devout admonitions from the ladies there; and they would fain have perfuaded him to acknowledge what they thought fo miraculous a deliverance, by embracing the Catholic faith, as they were pleafed to call it.   But they could not fucceed: for though no religion lay near his heart, yet he had too much of the fpirit of a gentleman, lightly to change that form of religion which he wore, as it were loofe about him; as well as too much good fenfe, to fwallow thofe monftrous abfurdities of popery, which immediately prefented themfelves to him, unac

quainted

quainted as he was with the niceties of the controverfy.

When his liberty was regained by an exchange of prifoners, and his health thoroughly eftablifhed, he was far from *rendering unto the Lord*, according to that wonderful difplay of divine mercy which he had experienced. I know very little of the particulars ~ of thofe wild, thoughtlefs, and wretched years, which lay between the nineteenth and the thirtieth of his life; except it be, that he frequently experienced the divide goodnefs in renewed inftances, particularly in preferving him in feveral hot military actions, in all which he never received fo much as a wound after this, forward as he was in tempting danger; and yet, that all thefe years were fpent in an entire alienation from God, and an eager purfuit of animal pleafure, as his fupreme good. The feries of *criminal amours*, in which he was almoft inceffantly engaged during this time, muft probably have afforded fome remarkable adventures and occurrences; but the memory of them is perifhed. Nor do I think it unworthy notice here, that amidft all the intimacy of our friendfhip, and the many hours of cheerful as well as ferious converfe which we fpent together, I never remember to have heard him fpeak of any

of

of thefe intrigues, otherwife than in the general, with deep and folemn abhorrence. This I the rather mention, as it feemed a moft genuine proof of his unfeigned repentance; which I think there is great reafon to fufpect, when people feem to take a pleafure in relating and defcribing fcenes of vicious indulgence, which yet they profefs to have difapproved and forfaken.

Amidft all thefe pernicious wanderings from the paths of religion, virtue, and happinefs, he approved himfelf fo well in his military character, that he was made a Lieutenant in that year, viz. 1706: And I am told, he was very quickly after promoted to a Cornet's commiffion in Lord Stair's regiment of the Scots Greys; and on the 31ft of January, 1714-15, was made Captain-Lieutenant in Col. Ker's regiment of dragoons. He had the honor of being known to the Earl of Stair fome time before, and was made his Aid de Camp; and when, upon his Lordfhip's being appointed Ambaffador from his late Majefty to the court of France, he made fo fplendid an entrance into Paris, Capt. Gardiner was his mafter of the horfe; and I have been told that a great deal of the care of that admirably well adjufted ceremony fell upon him; fo that he gained great credit by the manner in which he con-

ducted

ducted it.   Under the benign influences of
his Lordfhip's favour, a Captain's commiffion was procured for him, dated July 22d,
1715, in the regiment of dragoons commanded by Col. Stanhope, (now Earl of
Harrington) and, in the year 1717, he was
advanced to the majority of that regiment ;
in which office he continued till it was re-
duced, on Nov. 10th, 1718 ; when he was
put out of commiffion.   But then his Majefty George I. was fo thoroughly apprifed
of his faithful and important fervices, that
he gave him his fign manual, entitling him
to the firft majority that fhould become vacant in any regiment of horfe or dragoons,
which happened about five years after, to
be in Croft's regiment of dragoons, in which
he received a commiffion, dated June 1ft,
1724; and on the 20th of July the fame year,
he was made a Major of an older regiment,
commanded by the Earl of Stair.

As I am now fpeaking of fo many of his
military preferments, I will difpatch the account of them by obferving, that on the 24th
of January, 1729-30, he was advanced to
the rank of Lieutenant-Colonel in the fame
regiment, long under the command of Lord
Cadogan ; with whofe friendfhip this brave
and vigilant officer was alfo honoured for
many years.   And he continued in this

rank, and regiment, till the 19th of April, 1743, when he received a Colonel's commiſſion over a regiment of dragoons, lately commanded by Brigadier Bland; at the head of which he valiantly fell, in the defence of his Sovereign and his country, about two years and a half after he received it.

We will now return to that period of his life which paſſed at Paris, the ſcene of ſuch remarkable and important events. He continued (if I remember right) ſeveral years under the roof of the brave and generous Earl of Stair ; to whom he endeavoured to approve himſelf by every inſtance of diligent and faithful ſervice. And his lordſhip gave no inconſiderable proof of the dependence which he had upon him, when, in the beginning of the year 1715, he entruſted him with the important diſpatches, relating to a diſcovery, which, by a ſeries of admirable policy, he had made, of a deſign which the French King was then forming, for invading Great Britain in favour of the Pretender ; in which the French apprehended they were ſo ſecure of ſucceſs, that it ſeemed a point of friendſhip in one of the chief counſellors of that court, to diſſuade a dependant of his from accepting ſome employment under his Britannic Majeſty, when propoſed by his envoy there ; becauſe it was ſaid, that .

in

in lefs than fix weeks there would be a *rev-olution*, in favour of what they called the family of the .Stuarts. The Captain dif-patched his journey with the utmoft fpeed ; a variety of circumftances happily concur-red to accelerate it ; and they, who remem-ber how foon the regiments which that e-mergency required were raifed and armed, will, I doubt not, efteem it a memorable in-ftance, both of the moft cordial zeal in the friends of the government, and of the grac-ious care of Divine Providence, over the houfe of Hanover, and the Britifh liberties, fo infeparably connected with its intereft.

While Capt. Gardiner was at London, in one of the journies he made upon this occa-fion, he, with that franknefs which was nat-ural to him, and which in thofe days was not always under the moft prudent reftraint, ventured to predict, from what he knew of the bad ftate of the French King's health, that he would not live fix weeks. This was made known by fome fpies who were at St. James's, and came to be reported at the court of Verfailles ; for he received letters from fome friends at Paris, advifing him not to return thither, unlefs he could reconcile himfelf to a lodging in the Baftile. But he was foon free from that apprehenfion ; for, if I miftake not, before half that time was
accomplifhed,

accomplifhed, Lewis XIV. died ;* and, it is
generally thought, his death was haftened by
a very accidental circumftance, which had
fome reference to the Captain's prophecy.
For the laft time he ever dined in public,
which was a very little while after the report of it had been made there, he happened
to difcover our Britifh Envoy among the
fpectators. The penetration of this illuftrious perfon was too great, and his attachment to the intereft of his royal mafter too
well known, not to render him very difagreeable to that crafty and tyrannical prince,
whom God had fo long fuffered to be the
difgrace of monarchy, and the fcourge of
Europe. He at firft appeared very languid,
as indeed he was ; but on cafting his eye
upon the Earl of Stair, he affected to appear
before him in a much better ftate of health
than he really was ; and therefore, as if he
had been awakened on a fudden from fome
deep reverie, immediately put himfelf into
an erect pofture, called up a laboured vivac-
ity into his countenance, and eat much more
heartily than was by any means advifable,
repeating it two or three times to a noble-
man then in waiting, " Methinks I eat very
well, for a man who is to die fo foon."†

But

* September 1ft, 1715.
† Il me femble, que je ne mange pas mal pour un
homme qui devoit mourir fi tôt.

But this inroad upon that regularity of living, which he had for some time observed, agreed so ill with him, that he never recovered this meal, but died in less than a fortnight. This gave occasion for some humorous people to say, that old Lewis, after all, was killed by a Briton. But if this story be true, which I think there can be no room to doubt, as the Colonel, from whom I have often heard it, though absent, could scarce be misinformed) it might more properly be said, that he fell by his own vanity ; in which view I thought it so remarkable, as not to be unworthy a place in these memoirs.

The Captain quickly returned, and continued with small interruptions at Paris, at least till the year 1720, and how much longer I do not certainly know. The Earl's favour and generosity made him easy in his affairs, though he was, as has been observed before, part of the time out of commission, by breaking the regiment to which he belonged, of which before he was Major. This was, in all probability, the gayest part of his life, and the most criminal. Whatever wise and good examples he might find in the family where he had the honor to reside, it is certain that the French court, during the regency of the Duke of Orleans, was one of the most dissolute under heaven. What, by a wretched a wretched abuse of language, have been called *intrigues of love and gallantry*, were so entirely to the Major's then degenerate taste, that if not the whole *businefs*, at least the whole *happinefs* of his life confifted in them ; and he had now too much leifure, for one who was so prone to abufe it.   His fine conftitution, than which perhaps there was hardly ever a better, gave him great opportunities of indulging himfelf in thefe exceffes ; and his good fpirits enabled him to purfue his pleafures of every kind, in so alert and fprightly a manner, that multitudes envied him, and called him by a dreadful kind of compliment, the *happy rake*.

Yet ftill the checks of confcience, and some remaining principles of so good an education, would break in upon his moft licentious hours ; and I particularly remember he told me, that when some of his diffolute companions were once congratulating him on his diftinguifhed felicity, a dog happening at that time to come into the room, he could not forbear groaning inwardly, and faying to himfelf, " Oh that I were that dog !" Such then was his happinefs ; and fuch perhaps is that of hundreds more, who bear themfelves higheft in the contempt of religion, and glory in that infamous fervitude which they affect to call liberty. But
                                                thefe

thefe remonftrances of reafon and confcience were in vain ; and, in fhort, he carried things fo far, in this wretched part of his life, that I am well affured, fome fober Englifh gentleman, who made no great pretences to religion, how agreeable foever he might have been to them on other accounts, rather declined than fought his company, as fearing they might have been infnared and corrupted by it.

Yet I cannot find, that in thefe moft abandoned days, he was fond of drinking. Indeed he never had any natural relifh for that kind of intemperance, from which he ufed to think a manly pride might be fufficient to preferve perfons of fenfe and fpirit : as by it they gave up every thing that diftinguifhes them from the meaneft of their fpecies, or indeed from animals the moft below it.   So that, if he ever fell into any exceffes of this kind, it was merely out of complaifance to his company, and that he might not appear ftiff and fingular.   His frank, obliging, and generous temper, procured him many friends ; and thefe principles, which rendered him amiable to others, not being under the direction of true wifdom and piety, fometimes made him, in the ways of living he purfued, more uneafy to himfelf, than he might perhaps have been if he

could

could entirely have outgrown them ; efpecially as he was never a *fceptic* in his principles, but ftill retained a fecret apprehenfion, that natural and revealed religion, though he did not much care to think of either, were founded in truth.   And with this conviction, his notorious violations of the moft effential precepts of both, could not but occafion fome fecret mifgivings of heart.   His continual neglect of the great Author of his being, of whofe perfections he could not doubt, and to whom he knew himfelf to be under daily and perpetual obligations, gave him, in fome moments of involuntary reflection, inexpreffible remorfe ; and this, at times, wrought upon him to fuch a degree, that he refolved he would attempt to pay him fome acknowledgments.   Accordingly for a few mornings he did it ; repeating in retirement fome paffages out of the Pfalms, and perhaps other fcriptures, which he ftill retained in his memory ; and owning, in a few ftrong words, the many mercies and deliverances he had received, and the ill returns he had made for them.

I find, among the other papers tranfmitted to me, the following verfes, which I have heard him repeat, as what had impreffed him a good deal in his unconverted ftate : and as I fuppofe they did fomething towards

D   fetting

fetting him on this effort towards devotion, and might probably furnifh out a part of thefe orifons, I hope I need make no apology to my reader for inferting them, efpecially as I do not recollect that I have feen them any where elfe.

> Attend, my foul! the early birds infpire
> My grov'ling thoughts with pure celeftial fire :
> They from their temp'rate fleep awake, and pay
> Their thankful anthems for the new born day.
> See, how the tuneful lark is mounted high,
> And, poet like, falutes the eaftern fky !
> He warbles through the fragrant air his lays,
> And feems the beauties of the morn to praife.
> But man, more void of gratitude, awakes,
> And gives no thanks for the fweet reft he takes ;
> Looks on the glorious fun's new kindled flame,
> Without one thought of him from whom it came.
> The wretch unhallow'd does the day begin ;
> Shakes off his fleep, but fhakes not off his fin.

But thefe ftrains were too devout to continue long in a heart as yet quite unfanctified : for how readily foever he could repeat fuch acknowledgments of the divine power, prefence, and goodnefs, and own his own follies and faults ; he was ftopt fhort by the remonftrances of his confcience, as to the flagrant abfurdity of confeffing fins he did not defire to forfake, and of pretending to praife God for his mercies, when he did not
endeavour

endeavour to live to his fervice, and to behave in fuch a manner as gratitude, if fincere, would plainly dictate.   A model of
devotion, where fuch fentiments made no
part, his good fenfe could not digeft ; and
the ufe of fuch language before an heart
fearching God, merely as an hypocritical
form, while the fentiments of his foul were
contrary to it, juftly appeared to him fuch
daring profanenefs, that, irregular as the
ftate of his mind was, the thought of it ftruck
him with horror.   He therefore determined
to make no more attempts of this fort ; and
was perhaps one of the firft that deliberately laid afide prayer, from fome fenfe of
God's omnifcience, and fome natural principle of honour and confcience.

   Thefe fecret debates with himfelf, and in-
effectual efforts, would fometimes return :
but they were overborne, again and again,
by the force of temptation ; and it is no
wonder, that in confequence of them his
heart grew yet harder.   Nor was it foftened, or awakened, by fome very memorable
deliverances, which at this time he received.
He was in extreme danger by a fall from his
horfe, as he was riding poft, (I think in the
ftreets of Calais) when going down a hill,
the horfe threw him over his head, and
pitched over him ; fo that, when he rofe, the
                                      beaft

beaſt lay beyond him, and almoſt dead. Yet though he received not the leaſt harm, it made no ſerious impreſſion on his mind. In his return from England in the packet boat, (if I remember right, but a few weeks after the former accident) a violent ſtorm, that drove them up to Harwich, toſſed them from thence for ſeveral. hours in a dark night, on the coaſt of Holland, and brought them into ſuch extremity, that the Captain of the veſſel urged him to go to prayers immediately, if he ever intended to do it at all ; for he concluded, they would in a few minutes be at the bottom of the ſea. In this circumſtance he did pray, and that very fervently too : And it was very remarkable, that while he was crying to God for deliverance, the wind fell, and quickly after they arrived at Calais. But the Major was ſo little affected with what had befallen him, that when ſome of his gay friends, on hearing the ſtory, rallied him upon the efficacy of his prayers, he excuſed himſelf from the ſcandal of being thought much in earneſt, by ſaying, " that it was at midnight, an hour " when his good mother and aunt were a- " ſleep ; or elſe he ſhould have left that part " of the buſineſs to them." A ſpeech which I ſhould not have mentioned, but as it ſhews in ſo lively a view the wretched ſituation of

his

his mind at that time, though his great deliverance from the power of darkneſs was
then nearly approaching.   He recounted
theſe things to me with the greateſt humility, as ſhewing how utterly unworthy he was
of that miracle of divine grace, by which he
was quickly after brought to ſo true, and ſo
prevalent a ſenſe of religion.

And now I am come to that aſtoniſhing
part of his ſtory, the account of *his converſion;* which I cannot enter upon without
aſſuring the reader, that I have ſometimes
been tempted to ſuppreſs many circumſtances of it; not only as they may ſeem in-
credible to ſome, and enthuſiaſtical to others, but as I am very ſenſible they are liable
to great abuſes; which was the reaſon that he
gave me for concealing the moſt extraordinary from many perſons to whom he mentioned ſome of the reſt.   And I believe it
was this, together with the deſire of avoiding every thing that might look like oſtenta-
tion on this head, that prevented his leaving
a written account of it; though I have often intreated him to do it : as I particularly
remember I did in the very laſt letter I ever
wrote him; and pleaded the poſſibility of
his falling amidſt thoſe dangers, to which I
knew his valour might in ſuch circumſtances
naturally expoſe him.   I was not ſo happy

as to receive any anfwer to this letter, which reached him but a few days before his death : nor can I certainly fay, whether he had, or had not, complied with my requeft ; as it is very poffible a paper of that kind, if it were written, might be loft, amidft the ravages which the rebels made, when they plundered Bankton.

The ftory however was fo remarkable, that I had little reafon to apprehend I fhould ever forget it ; and yet, to guard againft all contingencies of that kind, I wrote it down that very evening, as I had heard it from his own mouth : and I have now before me the memoirs of that converfation, dated Auguft 14, 1739, which conclude with thefe words, (which I added, that if we fhould both have died that night, the world might not have loft this edifying and affecting hiftory, or have wanted any atteftation of it I was capable of giving :) " N. B. I have written down " this account with all the exactnefs I am " capable of, and could fafely take an oath " of it as to the truth of every circumftance, " to the beft of my remembrance, as the " Colonel related it to me a few hours ago." I do not know that I had reviewed this paper fince I wrote it, till I fet myfelf thus publicly to record this extraordinary fact ; but I find it punctually to agree with what

I have

I have often related from my memory, which
I charged carefully with fo wonderful and
important a fact.   It is with all folemnity
that I now deliver it down to pofterity as in
the fight and prefence of God, and I chufe
deliberately to expofe myfelf to thofe fevere
cenfures which the haughty, but empty,
fcorn of *infidelity*, or principles nearly approaching it, and effectually doing its pernicious work, may very probably dictate
upon the occafion, rather than to fmother a
relation which may, in the judgment of my
confcience, be like to conduce fo much to
the glory of God, the honour of the gofpel,
and the good of mankind.   One thing more
I will only premife, that I hope none who
have heard the Colonel himfelf fpeak fomething of this wonderful fcene, will be furprifed if they find fome new circumftances
here ; becaufe he affured me, at the time he
firft gave me the whole narration, which was
in the very room in which I now write, that
he had never imparted it fo fully to any man
living before.   Yet at the fame time he gave
me full liberty to communicate it, to whom-
foever I fhould in my confcience judge it
might be ufeful to do it, whether before, or
after his death.   Accordingly I did, while
he was alive, recount almoft every circumftance I am now going to write, to feveral
                                      pious

pious friends; referring them at the same
time to the Colonel himself, whenever they
might have an opportunity of seeing or writing to him, for a farther confirmation of what
I told them, if they judged it requisite.
They *glorified God in him*; and I humbly
hope many of my readers will also do it.
They will soon perceive the reason of so
much caution in my introduction to this
story, for which therefore I shall make no
further apology.*

This memorable event happened towards
the middle of July, 1719; but I cannot be
exact as to the day. The Major had spent
the evening (and if I mistake not it was the
Sabbath) in some gay company, and had an
unhappy assignation with a married woman,
of what rank or quality I did not particularly

* It is no small satisfaction to me, since I wrote this, to
have received a letter from the Rev. Mr. Spears, minister
of the gospel at Bruntisland, dated January 14, 1746-7, in
which he relates to me this whole story, as he had it from
the Colonel's own mouth, about four years after he gave
me the narration.   There is not a single circumstance, in
which either of our narrations disagree; and every one of
the particulars in mine, which seem most astonishing, are
attested by this, and sometimes in stronger words; one
only excepted, on which I shall add a short remark when
I come to it.   As this letter was written near Lady Frances
Gardiner, at her desire, and attended with a postscript
from her own hand, this is, in effect, a sufficient attestation
how agreeable it was to those accounts which she must
have often heard the Colonel give of this matter.

ly inquire, whom he was to attend exactly at twelve. The company broke up about eleven; and not judging it convenient to anticipate the time appointed, he went into his chamber to kill the tedious hour, perhaps with fome amufing book, or fome other way. But it very accidentally happened, that he took up a religious book, which his good mother or aunt had, without his knowledge, flipped into his portmanteau. It was called, if I remember the title exactly, *The Chriftian Soldier, or Heaven taken by Storm;* and was written by Mr. Thomas Watfon. Guefling by the title of it, that he fhould find fome phrafes of his own profeffion fpiritualized, in a manner which he thought might afford him fome diverfion, he refolved to dip into it; but he took no ferious notice of any thing he read in it: And yet, while this book was in his hand, an impreffion was made upon his mind, (perhaps God only knows how) which drew after it a train of the moft important and happy confequences.

There is indeed a poffibility, that while he was fitting in this attitude, and reading in this carelefs and profane manner, he might fuddenly fall afleep, and only *dream* of what he apprehended he faw. But nothing can be more certain, than that when he gave me

this

this relation, he judged himfelf to have been as broad awake, during the whole time, as he ever was in any part of his life ; and he mentioned it to me feveral times afterwards, as what undoubtedly paffed, not only in his imagination, but before his eyes.*

He thought he faw an unufual blaze of light fall on the book while he was reading, which he at firft imagined might happen by fome accident in the candle.   But lifting up his eyes, he apprehended, to his extreme amazement, that there was before him, as it were fufpended in the air, a vifible repre_fentation of the Lord Jefus Chrift upon the crofs, furrounded on all fides with a glory ; and was impreffed, as if a voice, or fome_thing equivalent to a voice, had come to him, to this effect, for he was not confident as to the very words, " Oh, finner ! did I fuffer

* Mr. Spears, in the letter mentioned above, where he introduces the Colonel telling his own ftory, has thefe words : " All of a fudden there was prefented in a very " lively manner, *to my view* or *to my mind*, a reprefenta- " tion of my glorious Redeemer," &c.   And this gentle- man adds, in a parenthefis, " It was fo lively and ftriking, " that he could not tell whether it was to his bodily eyes, " or to thofe of his mind."   This makes me think, that what I had faid to him on the phenomena of vifions, ap- paritions, &c. (as being, when moft real, fupernatural im- preffions on the imagination, rather than attended with any external object) had fome influence upon him.   Yet ftill it is evident, he looked upon this *as a vifion,* whether it were before the eyes or in the mind, and not *as a dream.*

suffer this for thee, and are these the returns ?" But whether this was an audible
voice, or only a ftrong impreffion on his
mind equally ftriking, he did not feem very
confident ; though, to the beft of my remembrance, he rather judged it to be the
former. Struck with fo amazing a phenomenon as this, there remained hardly any life
in him, fo that he funk down in the arm
chair, in which he fat, and continued, he
knew not exactly how long, infenfible ;
(which was one circumftance that made me
feveral times take the liberty to fuggeft, that
he might poffibly be all this while afleep :)
But however that were, he quickly after
opened his eyes, and faw nothing more than
ufual.

It may eafily be fuppofed, he was in no
condition to make any obfervation upon the
time in which he had remained in an infenfible ftate ; nor did he, throughout the remainder of the night, once recollect that
criminal and deteftable affignation which
had before engroffed all his thoughts. He
rofe in a tumult of paffions, not to be conceived, and walked to and fro in his chamber till he was ready to drop down, in unutterable aftonifhment and agony of heart ;
appearing to himfelf the vileft monfter in
the creation of God, who had all his life
time

time been *crucifying Chrift* afrefh by his fins, and now *faw*, as he affuredly believed, *by a miraculous vifion*, the horror of what he had done. With this was connected fuch a view, both of the majefty and goodnefs of God, as caufed him to lothe and *abhor him-felf*, and to *repent as in duft and afhes*. He immediately gave judgment againft himfelf, that he was moft juftly worthy of eternal damnation : He was aftonifhed that he had not been ftruck dead in the midft of his wickednefs : And, which I think deferves particular remark, though he affuredly believed that he fhould ere long be in hell, and fettled it as a point with himfelf for feveral months, that the wifdom and juftice of God did almoft neceffarily require, that fuch an enormous finner fhould be made an example of everlafting vengeance, and *a fpectacle*, as fuch, *both to angels and men*, fo that he hardly durft prefume to pray for pardon ; yet what he then fuffered, was not fo much from the fear of hell, though he concluded it would foon be his portion, as from a fenfe of that horrible ingratitude he had fhewn to the God of his life, and to that bleffed Redeemer, who had been in fo affecting a manner *fet forth as crucified before him*.

To

To this he refers in a letter, dated from Douglas, April 1, 1725, communicated to me by his lady,* but I know not to whom it was addreſſed. His words are theſe :—— " One thing relating to my converſion, and " a remarkable inſtance of the goodneſs of " God to me, *the chief of ſinners,* I do not " remember that I ever told to any other " perſon. It was this ; that after the *aſton-* " *iſhing ſight I had of my bleſſed Lord,* the " terrible condition in which I was, proceed- " ed not ſo much from the terrors of the " law, as from a ſenſe of having been ſo un- " grateful a monſter to him whom *I thought* " *I ſaw pierced* for my tranſgreſſions." I the rather inſert theſe words, as they evi-

dently

* N. B. Where I make any extracts as from Colonel Gardiner's letters, they are either from originals, which I have in my own hands, or from copies, which were tranſ- mitted to me from perſons of undoubted credit, chiefly by the Right Honourable the Lady Frances Gardiner, through the hand of the Rev. Mr. Webſter, one of the miniſters of Edinburgh. This I the rather mention, becauſe ſome let- ters have been brought to me as Colonel Gardiner's, con- cerning which I have not only been very dubious, but morally certain, that they could not have been written by him. I have alſo heard of many, who have been fond of aſſuring the world, that they were well acquainted with him, and were near him when he fell, whoſe reports have been moſt inconſiſtent with each other, as well as contrary to that teſtimony relating to the circumſtances of his death, which, on the whole, appeared to me beyond controverſy the moſt natural and authentic : From whence therefore I ſhall take my account of that affecting ſcene.

dently atteſt the circumſtance which may ſeem moſt amazing in this affair, and contain ſo expreſs a declaration of his own apprehenſion concerning it.

In this view it may naturally be ſuppoſ- that he paſſed the remainder of the night waking; and he could get but little reſt in ſeveral that followed. His mind was continually taken up in reflecting on the divine purity and goodneſs; the grace which had been propoſed to him in the Goſpel, and which he had rejected; the ſingular advantages he had enjoyed and abuſed; and the many favours of Providence which he had received, particularly in reſcuing him from ſo many imminent dangers of death, which he now ſaw muſt have been attended with ſuch dreadful and hopeleſs deſtruction.— The privileges of his education, which he had ſo much deſpiſed, now lay with an almoſt inſupportable weight on his mind; and the folly of that career of ſinful pleaſure, which he had ſo many years been running with deſperate eagerneſs and unworthy delight, now filled him with indignation againſt himſelf, and againſt the great deceiver, by whom (to uſe his own praiſe) he had been "ſo wretchedly and ſcandalouſly befooled." This he uſed often to expreſs in the ſtrongeſt terms; which I

ſhall

shall not repeat so particularly, as I cannot recollect some of them. But on the whole, it is certain, that by what passed before he left his chamber the next day, the whole frame and disposition of his soul was new modelled and changed ; so that he became and continued to the last day of his exemplary and truly christian life, the very reverse of what he had been before. A variety of particulars, which I am afterwards to mention, will illustrate this in the most convincing manner. But I cannot proceed to them, without pausing a while to adore so illustrious an instance of the power and freedom of divine grace, and intreating my reader seriously to reflect upon it, that his own heart may be suitably affected : For surely, if the truth of the fact be admitted in the lowest views in which it can be placed, (that is, supposing the first impression to have passed in a *dream)* it must be allowed to have been little, if any thing, less than *miraculous.* It cannot in the course of nature be imagined, how—*such a dream* should arise in a mind full of the most impure ideas and affections, and as he himself often plead, more alienated from the thoughts of a *crucified Saviour,* than from any other object that can be conceived : Nor can we surely suppose it should, without a mighty energy of
the

the divine power, be effectual to produce
not only fome tranfient flow of paffion, but
fo entire and fo permanent a change in character and conduct.

On the whole, therefore, I muft beg leave
to exprefs my own fentiments of the matter,
by repeating on this occafion what I wrote
feveral years ago, in my eighth fermon on
Regeneration, in a paffage dictated chiefly by
the circumftantial knowledge which I had
of this amazing ftory, and methinks fufficiently vindicated by it, if it ftood entirely
alone ; which yet, I muft take the liberty to
fay, it does not : For I hope the world will
be particularly informed, that there is at
leaft a fecond, that very nearly approaches
it, whenever the eftablifhed church of England fhall lofe one of its brighteft living ornaments, and one of the moft ufeful members, which that, or perhaps any other Chriftian communion, can boaft : In the mean
time, may his exemplary life be long continued, and his zealous miniftry abundantly
profpered ! I beg my reader's pardon for
this digreffion. The paffage I referred to
above is remarkably, though not equally,
applicable to both the cafes, as it ftands in
page 263, of the firft edition, under that
head where I am fhewing, that God fometimes accomplifhes the great work of which

we

we fpeak, by fecret and immediate impreffions on the mind.   After preceding illuf-
trations, there are the following words, on
which the Colonel's converfion will throw
the jufteft light : " Yea, I have known thofe
" of diftinguifhed genius, polite manners,
" and great experience in human affairs,
" who, after having outgrown all the im-
" preffions of a religious education ; after
" having been hardened, rather than fubdu-
" ed, by the moft fingular mercies, even va-
" rious, repeated and aftonifhing deliver-
" ances, which have appeared to themfelves
" no lefs than miraculous ; after having liv-
" ed for years *without God in the world*, no-
" torioufly corrupt themfelves, and labour-
" ing to the utmoft to corrupt others, have
" been ftopt on a fudden in the full career
" of their fin, and have felt fuch rays of the
" divine prefence, and of redeeming love,
" darting in upon their minds, almoft like
" lightning from heaven, as have at once
" rouzed, overpowered, and transformed
" them : So that they have come out of
" their fecret chambers with an irreconcile-
" able enmity to thofe vices, to which, when
" they entered them, they were the tameft
" and moft abandoned flaves ; and have ap-
" peared from that very hour the votaries,
" the patrons, the champions of religion ;
and

" and after a courſe of the moſt reſolute
" attachment to it, in ſpite of all the reaſon-
" ings or the railleries, the importunities or
" the reproaches, of its enemies, they have
" continued to this day ſome of its brighteſt
" ornaments : A change, which I behold
" with equal wonder and delight, and which,
" if a nation ſhould join in deriding it, I
" would adore as the finger of God."

The mind of Major Gardiner continued
from this remarkable time till towards the
end of October, that is, rather more than
three months, but eſpecially the two firſt of
them, in as extraordinary a ſituation as one
can well imagine. He knew nothing of the
joys ariſing from a ſenſe of pardon ; but, on
the contrary, for the greater part of that
time, and with very ſhort intervals of hope
toward the end of it, took it for granted, that
he muſt, in all probability, quickly periſh.
Nevertheleſs, he had ſuch a ſenſe of the evil
of ſin, of the goodneſs of the Divine Being,
and of the admirable tendency of the Chriſtian revelation, that he reſolved to ſpend the
remainder of his life, while God continued
him out of hell, in as rational and as uſeful
a manner as he could ; and to continue caſt-
ing himſelf at the feet of divine mercy every
day, and often in a day, if peradventure
there might be hope of pardon, of which all
                                    that

that he could fay was, that he *did not abfo-*
lutely defpair.   He had at that time fuch a
fenfe of the degeneracy of his own heart,
that he hardly durft form any determinate
refolution againft fin, or pretend to engage
himfelf by any vow in the prefence of God;
but he was continually crying to him that he
would deliver him from the bondage of corruption.   He perceived in himfelf a moft
furprifing alteration with regard to the difpofitions of his heart; fo that, though he
felt little of the delight of religious duties,
he extremely defired opportunities of being
engaged in them; and thofe licentious
pleafures, which had before been his heaven,
were now abfolutely his averfion.   And indeed, when I confider how habitual all thofe
criminal indulgences were grown to him,
and that he was now in the prime of life,
and all this while in high health too, I cannot but be aftonifhed to reflect upon it, that
he fhould be fo wonderfully *fanctified in body,*
as well as *in foul and fpirit,* as that, for all
the future years of his life, he, from that
hour, fhould find fo conftant a difinclination
to, and abhorrence of, thofe criminal fenfualities, to which he fancied he was before fo
invincibly impelled by his very conftitution, that he was ufed ftrangely to think,
and to fay, that Omnipotence itfelf could not
reform

reform him, without deftroying that body, and giving him another.*

Nor was he only delivered from that bondage of corruption, which had been ha-bitual to him for fo many years, but felt in his

* Mr. Spears expreffes this wonderful circumftance in thefe remarkable words : " I was (faid the Colonel to me) " effectually cured ot all inclination to that *fin* I was fo " ftrongly addicted to, that I thought nothing but fhooting " me through the head could have cured me of it ; and all " defire and inclination to it was removed, as entirely as " if I had been a fucking child ; nor did the temptation " return to this day." Mr. Webfter's words on the fame fubject are thefe : " One thing I have heard the Colonel " frequently fay, that he was much addicted to impurity " before his acquaintance with religion ; but that, fo foon " as he was enlightened from above, he felt *the power of the* " *Holy Ghoft* changing his nature fo wonderfully, that his " fanctification in this refpect feemed more remarkable " than in any other." On which that worthy perfon makes this very reafonable reflection : " So thorough a " change of fuch a polluted nature, evidenced by the moft " unblemifhed walk and converfation for a long courfe of " years, demonftrates indeed *the power of the higheft*, and " leaves no room to doubt of its reality." Mr. Spears fays, this happened in three days time : But from what I can recollect, all that the Colonel could mean by that expreffion, if he ufed it, as I conclude he did, was, that he began to make the obfervation in the fpace of three days ; whereas, during that time, his thoughts were fo taken up with the wonderful views prefented to his mind, that he did not immediately attend to it. If he had within the firft three days any temptation to feek fome eafe from the anguifh of his mind, in returning to former fenfualities, it is a circumftance he did not mention to me ; and by what I can recollect of the ftrain of his difcourfe, he intimated, if he did not ex-prefs, the contrary.

his breaſt ſo contrary a diſpoſition, that he was grieved to ſee human nature, in thoſe to whom he was moſt entirely a ſtranger, proſtituted to ſuch low and contemptible purſuits.   He therefore exerted his natural courage in a very new kind of combat, and became an open advocate for religion, in all its principles, ſo far as he was acquainted with them, and all its precepts, relating to ſobriety, righteouſneſs, and godlineſs.   Yet he was very deſirous and cautious, that he might not run into an extreme, and made it one of his firſt petitions to God, the very day after theſe amazing impreſſions had been wrought in his mind, that he might not be ſuffered to behave with ſuch an affected ſtiffneſs and precifeneſs, as would lead others about him into miſtaken notions of religion, and expoſe it to reproach or ſuſpicion, as if it were an unlovely or uncomfortable thing. For this reaſon he endeavoured to appear as cheerful in converſation as he conſcientiouſly could ; though, in ſpite of all his precautions, ſome traces of that deep inward ſenſe which he had of his guilt and miſery, would at times appear.   He made no ſecret of it, however, that his views were entirely changed, though he concealed the particular circumſtances attending that change.   He told his moſt intimate companions freely, that he

had

had reflected on the course of life in which he had so long joined them, and found it to be folly and madness, unworthy a rational creature, and much more unworthy persons calling themselves Christians. And he set up his standard, upon all occasions, against principles of infidelity, and practices of vice, as determinately, and as boldly, as ever he displayed or planted *his colours*, when he bore them with so much honour in the field.

I cannot forbear mentioning one struggle of this kind, which he described to me, with a large detail of circumstances, the first day of our acquaintance. There was at that time in Paris a certain lady, whose name, then well known in the grand and the gay world, I must beg leave to conceal, who had imbibed the principles of Deism, and valued herself much upon being an avowed advocate for them. The Major, with his usual frankness, though I doubt not with that politeness of manners which was so habitual to him, and which he retained throughout his whole life, answered her, like a man who perfectly saw through the fallacy of her arguments, and was grieved to the heart for her delusion. On this she briskly challenged him to debate the matter at large, and to fix upon a day for that purpose, when he should dine with her, attended with any *Clergyman*

gyman he might chufe, whether of the Proteftant or Catholic communion.   A fenfe of
duty would not allow him to decline this
challenge ; and yet he had no fooner accepted it, but he was thrown into great per-
plexity and diftrefs, left being (as I remember he expreffed it, when he told me the
ftory) only a *Chriftian of fix weeks old,* he
fhould prejudice fo good a caufe, by his un-
fkilful manner of defending it.   However,
he fought his refuge in earneft, and repeated
prayers to God, that he, who can *ordain*
ftrength, and perfect praife, out of the mouth
of babes and fucklings, would gracioufly enable him, on this occafion, to vindicate his
truths in a manner which might carry conviction along with it.   He then endeavoured to marfhal the arguments in his own mind
as well as he could ; and apprehending that
he could not fpeak with fo much freedom
before a number of perfons, efpecially before
fuch whofe province he might in that cafe
feem to invade, if he had not devolved the
principal part of the difcourfe upon them,
he eafily admitted the apology of a Clergyman or two, to whom he mentioned the affair, and waited on the lady alone upon the
day appointed.   But his heart was fo fet
upon the bufinefs, that he came earlier than
he was expected, and time enough to have
                                        two

two hours difcourfe before dinner ; nor did
he at all decline having two young perfons,
nearly related to the lady, prefent during
the conference.

The Major opened it, with a view of fuch
arguments for the Chriftian religion as he
had digefted in his own mind, to prove that
the Apoftles were not miftaken themfelves,
and that they could not have intended to
impofe upon us, in the accounts they give of
the grand facts they atteft ; with the truth
of which facts, that of the Chriftian religion
is moft apparently connected.   And it was
a great encouragement to him, to find, that
unaccuftomed as he was to difcourfes of this
nature, he had an unufual command, both
of thought and expreffion ; fo that he recollected, and uttered every thing, as he could
have wifhed.   The lady heard with attention ; and though he paufed between every
branch of the argument, fhe did not interrupt the courfe of it, till he told her he had
finifhed his defign, and waited for her reply.
She then produced fome of her objections,
which he took up and canvaffed in fuch a
manner, that at length fhe burft out into
tears, allowed the force of his arguments and
replies, and appeared, for fome time after,
fo deeply impreffed with the converfation,
that it was obferved by feveral of her friends :

And

And there is reafon to believe, that the impreffion continued, at leaft fo far as to prevent her from ever appearing under the
character of an unbeliever or a fceptic.

This is only one fpecimen among many,
of the battles he was almoft daily called out
to fight in the caufe of religion and virtue ;
with relation to which I find him expreffing
himfelf thus, in a letter to Mrs. Gardiner,
his good mother, dated from Paris, the 25th
of January following, that is, 1719-20, in
anfwer to one, in which fhe had warned him
to expect fuch trials : " I have, (fays he)
" already met with them, and am obliged to
" fight and difpute every inch of ground :
" But all thanks and praife to the great *Cap-*
" *tain of my falvation*, he fights for me ;
" and then it is no wonder, that I come off
" *more than conqueror ;*" by which laft expreffion I fuppofe he meant to infinuate,
that he was ftrengthened and eftablifhed,
rather than overborne by this oppofition.
Yet it was not immediately, that he gained
fuch fortitude. He has often told me how
much he felt in thofe days, of the emphafis
of thofe well chofen words of the Apoftle,
in which he ranks the *trial of cruel mockings,*
with fcourgings, and bonds, and imprifon-
ments. The continual railleries with which
he was received, in almoft all companies

F   where

where he had been moſt familiar before, did
often diſtreſs him beyond meaſure ; ſo that
he has ſeveral times declared, he would
much rather have marched up to a battery
of the enemy's cannon, than have been o‑
bliged, ſo continually as he was, to face ſuch
artillery as this.   But like a brave ſoldier in
the firſt action wherein he is engaged, he
continued reſolute, though ſhuddering at
the terror of the aſſault ; and quickly over‑
came thoſe impreſſions, which it is not per‑
haps in nature wholly to avoid : And there‑
fore I find him in the letter referred to a‑
bove, which was written about half a year
after his converſion, " quite aſhamed to think
" of the uneaſineſs which theſe things once
" gave him."   In a word, he went on, as
every reſolute Chriſtian by divine grace may
do, till he turned ridicule and oppoſition in‑
to reſpect and veneration.

But this ſenſible triumph over theſe diffi‑
culties, was not till his Chriſtian experience
had been abundantly advanced by the bleſſ‑
ing of God on the ſermons he heard, partic‑
ularly in the Swiſs chapel, and on the many
hours which he ſpent in devout retirement,
pouring out his whole ſoul before God in
prayer.   He began, within about two
months after his firſt memorable change, to
perceive ſome ſecret dawnings of more
cheerful

cheerful hope, that vile as he faw himfelf to
be, (and I believe no words can exprefs how
vile that was) he might neverthelefs obtain
mercy through a Redeemer. And at length,
if I remember right, about the end of October,
1719, he found all the burthen of his
mind taken off at once, by the powerful impreffion
of that memorable fcripture upon
his mind ; ROM. iii. 25, 26. *Whom God
hath fet forth for a propitiation through faith
in his blood, to declare his righteoufnefs in the
remiffion of fins——that he might be juft, and
the juftifier of him that believeth in Jefus.*
He had ufed to imagine, that the juftice of
God required the damnation of fo enormous
a finner, as he faw himfelf to be : But now
he was made deeply fenfible, that the divine
juftice might be, not only vindicated, but
glorified, in faving him *by the blood of Jefus,*
even that *blood,* which *cleanfeth us from all
fin.* Then did he fee and feel the riches of
redeeming love and grace, in fuch a manner,
as not only engaged him, with the utmoft
pleafure and confidence to venture his foul
upon it ; but even fwallowed up, as it were,
his whole heart in the returns of love, which
from that bleffed time became the genuine
and delightful principle of his obedience,
and animated him *with an enlarged heart,
to run the way of God's commandments.* Thus

God

God was pleafed, (as he himfelf ufed to fpeak) in an hour *to turn his captivity.* All the terrors of his former ftate were changed into unutterable joy, which kept him almoft continually waking for three nights together, and yet refrefhed him as the nobleft of cordials. His expreffions, though naturally very ftrong, always feemed to be fwallowed up, when he would defcribe the feries of thought through which he now paffed, under the rapturous experience of that *joy unfpeakable, and full of glory,* which then feemed to overflow his very foul ; as indeed there was nothing he feemed to fpeak of with greater relifh. And though the firft ecftacies of it afterwards fubfided into a more calm and compofed delight, yet were the impreffions fo deep and fo permanent, that he affured me, on the word of a Chriftian and a friend, wonderful as it might feem, that for about feven years after this, he enjoyed almoft an *heaven upon earth.* His foul was fo continually filled with a fenfe of the love of God in Chrift, that it knew little interruption, but when neceffary converfe, and the duties of his ftation, called off his thoughts for a little time : and when they did fo, as foon as he was alone, the torrent returned into its natural channel again ; fo that, from the minute of his awakening in the morning,

his

his heart was rifing to God, and triumphing in him; and thefe thoughts attended him through all the fcenes of life, till he lay down on his bed again, and a fhort paren-thefis of fleep (for it was but a very fhort one that he allowed himfelf) invigorated his animal powers, for renewing them with greater intenfenefs and fenfibility.

I fhall have an opportunity of illuftrating this in the moft convincing manner below, by extracts from feveral letters which he wrote to intimate friends during this happy period of time : letters which breathe a fpirit of fuch fublime and fervent piety, as I have feldom met with any where elfe. In thefe circumftances, it is no wonder, that he was greatly delighted with Dr. Watts's im-itation of the 126th Pfalm ; fince it may be queftioned, whether there ever was a perfon, to whom the following ftanzas of it were more fuitable..

When God reveal'd his gracious name,
  And chang'd my mournful ftate,
My rapture feem'd a pleafing dream ;
  The grace appear'd fo great.

The world beheld the glorious change,
  And did thine hand confefs ;
My tongue broke out in unknown ftrains,
  And fung furprifing grace.

F 2   " Great

" Great is the work," my neighbors cry'd,
  And own'd the power divine :
" Great is the work," my heart reply'd,
  " And be the glory thine."

The Lord can change the darkeſt ſkies,
  Can give us day for night,
Make floods of ſacred ſorrow riſe
  To rivers of delight.

Let thoſe that ſow in ſadneſs, wait
  Till the fair harveſt come :
They ſhall confeſs their ſheaves are great,
  And ſhout the bleſſings home.

I have been ſo happy as to get the ſight of five original letters, which he wrote to his mother about this time ; which do, in a very lively manner, illuſtrate the ſurpriſing change made in the whole current of his thoughts, and temper of his mind.   Many of them were written in the moſt haſty manner, juſt as the courier who brought them was, perhaps unexpectedly, ſetting out ; and they relate chiefly to affairs, in which the public is not at all concerned : yet there is not one of them, in which he has not inſerted ſome warm and genuine ſentiment of religion.   And indeed it is very remarkable, that though he was pleaſed to honour me with a great many letters, and I have ſeen ſeveral more which he wrote to others, ſome

of

of them on journies, where he could have
but a few minutes at command, yet I cannot
recollect, that I ever faw any one, in which
there was not fome trace of piety.   And the
Rev. Mr. Webfter, who was employed to
review great numbers of them, that he might
felect fuch extracts as he fhould think proper
to communicate to me, has made the fame
obfervation.*

The Major, with great juftice, tells the
good lady his mother, "that when fhe faw
" him again, fhe would find the perfon in-
" deed the fame, but every thing elfe entire-
" ly changed."   And fhe might eafily have
perceived it of herfelf, by the whole tenor of
thofe letters, which every where breathe the
unaffected fpirit of a true Chriftian.   They
are taken up, fometimes with giving advice
and directions concerning fome pious and
charitable contributions ; one of which I
remember amounted to ten guineas, though,
as he was then out of commiffion, and had

not

* His words are thefe : " I have read over a vaft
" number of the Colonel's letters, and have not found
" any one of them, however fhort, and wrote in the
" moft paffing manner, even when pofting, but what is
" expreffive of the moft paffionate breathings towards
" his God and Saviour. If the letter confifts but of
" two fentences, religion is not forgot, which doubtlefs
" deferves to be carefully remarked, as the moft un-
" contefted evidence of a pious mind, ever under the
" warmeft impreffions of divine things."

not formerly been very frugal, it cannot be fuppofed he had much to fpare ; fometimes in fpeaking of the pleafure with which he attended fermons, and expected facramental opportunities ; and at other times, in exhorting her, eftablifhed as fhe was in religion, to labour after a yet more exemplary character and conduct, or in recommending her to the divine prefence and blefling, as well as himfelf to her prayers.   What fatisfaction fuch letters as thefe muft give to a lady of her diftinguifhed piety, who had fo long wept over this dear and amiable fon, as quite loft to God, and on the verge of final deftruction, it is not for me to defcribe, or indeed to conceive.   But haftily as thefe letters were written, only for private view, I will give a few fpecimens from them in his own words ; which will ferve to illuftrate, as well as confirm, what I have hinted above.

" I muft take the liberty," fays he, in a letter dated on the firft day of the new year, or according to the old ftile, Dec. 21, 1719, " to intreat you, that you would receive no " company on the Lord's day.   I know you " have a great many good acquaintance, with " whofe difcourfes one might be very well " edified : but as you cannot keep out, and " let in, whom you pleafe, the beft way, in " my humble opinion, will be to fee none."

In

In another, of Jan. 25, " I am happier than
" any one can imagine, except I could put
" him exactly in the fame fituation with
" myfelf; which is what the world cannot
" give, and no man ever attained it, unlefs it
" were from above." In another, dated
March 30, which was juft before a facrament
day, " Tomorrow, if it pleafe God, I fhall be
" happy ; my foul being to be fed with *the*
" *bread of life,* which came down from heav-
" en. I fhall be mindful of you all there."
In another of Jan. 29, he thus exprefTes that
indifference for worldly poffeffions, which
he fo remarkably carried through all the remainder of his life; " I know, the rich are
" only ftewards for the poor, and muft give
" an account for every penny ; therefore
" the lefs I have, the more eafy will it be to
" render a faithful account of it." And to
add no more from thefe letters at prefent, in
the conclufion of one of them he has thefe
comprehenfive and folemn words : " Now
" that he, who is the eafe of the afflicted, the
" fupport of the weak, the wealth of the
" poor, the teacher of the ignorant, the an-
" chor of the fearful, and the infinite reward
" of all faithful fouls, may pour out upon
" you all his richeft bleffings, fhall always be
" the prayer of him who is entirely your's,
" &c."

To

To this account of his correspondence with his excellent mother, I shall be glad to add a large view of another, to which she introduced him, with that reverend and valuable person, under whose pastoral care she was placed, I mean the justly celebrated Dr. Edmund Calamy, to whom she could not but early communicate the joyful news of her son's conversion. I am not so happy as to be possessed of the letters which passed between them, which I have reason to believe would make a curious and valuable collection : But I have had the pleasure of receiving, from my worthy and amiable friend, the Rev. Mr. Edmund Calamy, one of the letters which the Doctor, his father, wrote to the Major on this wonderful occasion. I perceive by the contents of it, that it was the first ; and indeed it is dated as early as the third of August, 1719, which must be but a few days after his own account dated August 4, N. S. could reach England. There is so much true religion and good sense in this paper, and the counsel it suggests may be so seasonable to other persons in circumstances which bear any resemblance to his, that I make no apology to my reader for inserting a large extract from it.

" Dear Sir, I conceive it will not much
" surprise you to understand that your good
" mother

" mother communicated to me your letter
" to her, dated Aug. 4, N. S. which brought
" her the news you conceived would be fo
" acceptable to her. I, who have often
" been a witnefs to her concern for you on
" a fpiritual account, can atteft with what
" joy this news was received by her, and im—
" parted to me as a fpecial friend, who fhe
" knew would bear a part with her on fuch
" an occafion. And indeed, if (as our Sav-
" iour intimates, Luke xv. 7, 10) *there is*, in
" fuch cafes, *joy in heaven*, and *among the*
" *angels of God*, it may well be fuppofed,
" that of a pious mother, who has fpent fo
" many prayers and tears upon you, and
" has, as it were, *travailed in birth with you*
" *again, till Chirft was formed in you*, could
" not be fmall. You may believe me if I
" add, that I alfo, as a common friend of
" her's and your's, and, which is much more,
" of the Prince of light, whom you now de-
" clare you heartily fall in with in oppofi-
" tion to that of the dark kingdom, could
" not but be tenderly affected with an ac-
" count of it under your own hand. My
" joy on this account was the greater, con-
" fidering the importance of your capacity,
" interefts, and profpects; which, in fuch
" an age as this, may promife moft happy
" confequences, on your heartily appearing
                                             " on

" on God's fide, and embarking in the in-
" tereft of our dear Redeemer. If I have
" hitherto at all remembered you *at the*
" *throne of grace,* at your good mother's de-
" fire, (which you.are pleafed to take notice
" of with fo much refpe&t) I can affure you
" I fhall henceforward be led to do it, with
" more concern and particularity, both by
" duty and inclination. And if I were ca-
" pable of giving you any little affiftance in
" the noble defign you are engaging in, by
" correfponding with you by letter, while
" you are at fuch a diftance, I fhould do it
" moft cheerfully. And, perhaps, fuch a
" motion may not be altogether unaccepta-
" ble : For I am inclinable to believe, that
" when fome, whom you are obliged to con-
" verfe with, obferve your behaviour fo dif-
" ferent from what it formerly was, and
" banter you upon it as mad and fanciful, it
" may be fome little relief to correfpond
" with one who will take a pleafure in heart-
" ening and encouraging you. And when
" a great many things frequently offer, in
" which confcience may be concerned, where
" duty may not always be plain, nor fuita-
" ble perfons to advife with at hand, it may
" be fome fatisfa&tion to you to correfpond
" with one, with whom you may ufe a friend-
" ly freedom in all fuch matters, and on
                                " whofe

" whofe fidelity you may depend. You
" may therefore command me in any of
" thefe refpe&ts, and I fhall take a pleafure in
" ferving you.   One piece of advice I fhall
" venture to give you, though your own
" good fenfe will make my enlarging upon
" it lefs needful, I mean, that you would,
" from your firft fetting out, carefully dif-
" tinguifh between the *effentials* of real re-
" ligion, and thofe things which are com-
" monly reckoned by its profeffors to belong
" to it.   The want of this diftin&tion has
" had very unhappy confequences from one
" age to another, and perhaps in none more
" than the prefent.   But your daily con-
" verfe with your Bible, which you mention,
" may herein give you great affiftance.   I
" move alfo, that fince infidelity fo much a-
" bounds, you would, not only by clofe and
" ferious confideration, endeavour to fettle
" yourfelf well in the fundamental principles
" of religion ; but alfo that, as opportunity
" offers, you would converfe with thofe
" books which treat moft judicioufly on the
" divine original of Chriftianity, fuch as
" Grotius, Abadie, Baxter, Bates, Du Plef-
" fis, &c. which may eftablifh you againft
" the cavils that occur in almoft all converfa-
" tions, and furnifh you with arguments
" which, when properly offered, may be of
G   "ufe

" ufe to make fome impreffions on others.
" But being too much ftraightened to en-
" large at prefent, I can only add, that if
" your hearty falling in with ferious religion
" fhould prove any hindrance to your ad-
" vancement in the world, (which I pray
" God it may not, unlefs fuch advancement
" would be a real fnare to you) I hope you
" will truft our Saviour's word, that it fhall
" be no difadvantage to you in the final if-
" fue : He has given you his word for it,
" MAT. xix. 29. upon which you may fafely
" depend ; and I am fatisfied, none, that
" ever did fo, at laft repented of it.   May
" you go on and profper, and the God of
" all grace and peace be with you."

I think it very evident from the contents
of this letter, that the Major had not imparted to his mother the moft fingular circumftances attending his converfion : And,
indeed, there was fomething fo peculiar in
them, that I do not wonder he was always
cautious in fpeaking of them, and, efpecially
that he was at firft much on the referve.   We
may alfo naturally reflect, that there feems to
have been fomething very providential in
this letter, confidering the debate in which
our illuftrious convert was fo foon engaged ;
for it was written but about three weeks before his conference with the lady above mentioned,

tioned, in the defence of Chriftianity ; or,
at leaft, before the appointment of it.   And
as fome of the books recommended by Dr.
Calamy, particularly Abadie and Du Pleffis,
were undoubtedly within his reach, (if our
Englifh advocates were not) this might, by
the divine blefling, contribute confiderably
towards arming him for that combat, in
which he came off with fuch happy fuccefs.
And as in this inftance, fo in many others,
they who will obferve the coincidence and
concurrence of things, may be engaged to
adore the wife conduct of providence in e-
vents, which, when taken fingly and by
themfelves, have nothing very remarkable
in them.

I think it was about this time, that this
refolute and exemplary Chriftian entered
upon that methodical manner of living,
which he purfued through fo many fucceeding years of his life, and I believe, generally, fo far as the broken ftate of his health
would allow it in his latter days, to the very
end of it.   He ufed conftantly to rife at
four in the morning, and to fpend his time
till fix in the fecret exercifes of devotion,
reading, meditation and prayer ; in which
laft he contracted fuch a fervency of fpirit,
as I believe few men living ever obtained.
This certainly tended very much to ftrength-
en

en that firm faith in God, and reverent animating fenfe of his prefence, for which he
was fo eminently remarkable, and which
carried him through the trials and fervices
of life, with fuch fteadinefs, and with fuch
activity ; for he indeed endured, and acted
as always *feeing Him who is invifible.*   If at
any time he was obliged to go out before fix
in the morning, he arofe proportionably
fooner ; fo that when a journey, or a march,
has required him to be on horfeback by
four, he would be at his devotions at fartheft
by two.   He likewife fecured time for retirement in an evening ; and that he might
have it the more at command, and be the
more fit to ufe it properly, as well as the
better able to rife early the next morning,
he generally went to bed about ten : And
during the time I was acquainted with him,
he feldom eat any fupper, but a mouthful
of bread with one glafs of wine.   In confequence of this, as well as of his admirably
good conftitution, and the long habit he
had formed, he required lefs fleep than moft
perfons I have known : And I doubt not
but his uncommon progrefs in piety was in
a great meafure owing to thefe refolute
habits of felf denial.

A life any thing like this, could not, to be
fure, be entered upon, in the midft of fuch

company

company as he had been accuſtomed to
keep, without great oppoſition, eſpecially,
as he did not entirely withdraw himſelf from
all the circle of cheerful converſation ; but
on the contrary, gave ſeveral hours every
day to it, left religion ſhould be reproach-
ed, as having made him moroſe.   He however, early began a practice, which to the
laſt day of his life he retained, of *reproving
vice and profaneuſs* ; and was never afraid
to debate the matter with any, under the
conſcioufneſs of ſuch ſuperiority in the
goodneſs of his cauſe.

A remarkable inſtance of this happened,
if I miſtake not, about the middle of the
year 1720, though I cannot be very exact
as to the date of the ſtory. It was however on his firſt return, to make any conſiderable abode in England, after this remarkable change.   He had heard, on the
other ſide of the water, that it was current-
ly reported among his companions at home,
that he was *ſtark mad* : A report, at which,
no reader, who knows *the wiſdom of the
world* in theſe matters, will be much ſurpriſed, any more than himſelf.   He concluded, therefore, that he ſhould have many
battles to fight, and was willing to diſpatch
the buſineſs as faſt as he could.   And therefore, being to ſpend a few days at the coun-

G 2   try

try houfe of a perfon of diftinguifhed rank, with whom he had been very intimate, (whofe name I do not remember that he told me, nor did I think it proper to enquire after it) he begged the favour of him that he would contrive matters fo, that a day or two after he came down, feveral of their former gay companions might meet at his Lordfhip's table : that he might have an opportunity of making his apology to them, and acquainting them with the nature and reafons of his change. It was accordingly agreed to ; and a pretty large company met on the day appointed, with previous notice that Major Gardiner would be there. A good deal of raillery paffed at dinner, to which the Major made very little anfwer. But when the cloth was taken away, and the fervants retired, he begged their patience for a few minutes, and then plainly and ferioufly told them, what notions he entertained of virtue and religion, and on what confiderations he had abfolutely determined, that by the grace of God he would make it the care and bufinefs of life, whatever he might lofe by it, and whatever cenfure and contempt he might incur. He well knew how improper it was in fuch company to relate the extraordinary manner in which he was awakened ; which they would

probably

probably have interpreted as a demonſtration of lunacy, againſt all the gravity and
ſolidity of his diſcourſe : But he contented
himſelf with ſuch a rational defence of a
righteous, ſober and godly life, as he knew
none of them could with any ſhadow of reaſon conteſt.   He then challenged them to
propoſe any thing they could urge, to prove
that a life of irreligion and debauchery was
preferable to the fear, love, and worſhip of
the eternal God, and a conduct agreeable to
the precepts of his goſpel.   And he failed
not to bear his teſtimony, from his own experience, (to one part of which many of
them had been witneſſes) that after having
run the wideſt round of ſenſual pleaſure,
with all the advantages the beſt conſtitution
and ſpirits could give him, he had never
taſted any thing that deſerved to be called
happineſs, till he had made religion his refuge and his delight.   He teſtified calmly
and boldly, the habitual ſerenity and peace
that he now felt in his own breaſt, (for the
moſt elevated delights he did not think fit to
plead, leſt they ſhould be eſteemed enthuſiaſm) and the compoſure and pleaſure with
which he looked forward to objects, which
the gayeſt ſinner muſt acknowledge to be
equally unavoidable and dreadful.

I know not what might be attempted by
ſome of the company in anſwer to this ; but
I well

I well remember he told me, the master of
the table, a person of a very frank and candid disposition, cut short the debate, and
said, " Come, let us call another cause : We
" thought this man mad, and he is in good
" earnest proving that we are so." On the
whole, this well judged circumstance saved
him a geat deal of future trouble. When
his former acquaintance observed, that he
was still conversable and innocently cheerful, and that he was immoveable in his reso-
lutions, they desisted from farther importunity. And he has assured me, that instead
of losing any one valuable friend by this
change in his character, he found himself
much more esteemed and regarded, by many
who could not persuade themselves to imitate his example.

I have not any memoirs of Col. Gardiner's life, or of any other remarkable event
befalling him in it, from the time of his return to England, till his marriage in the year
1726 ; except the extracts which have been
sent me from some letters, which he wrote to
his religious friends during this interval, and
which I cannot pass by without a more particular notice. It may be recollected, that
in consequence of the reduction of that regiment of which he was Major, he was out of
commission from Nov. 10th, 1718, to June
1st, 1724. And after he returned from
Paris,

Paris, I find all his letters, during this period, dated from London, where he continued
in communion with the Chriftian fociety
under the paftoral care of Dr. Calamy.   As
his good mother alfo belonged to the fame,
it is eafy to imagine it muft be an unfpeakable pleafure to her, to have fuch frequent
opportunities of converfing with fuch a fon,
of obferving in his daily conduct and difcourfes the bleffed effects of that change
which divine grace had made in his heart,
and of fitting down with him monthly at
that facred feaft, where Chriftians fo frequently enjoy the divineft entertainments
which they expect on this fide heaven.   I
the rather mention this ordinance, becaufe as
this excellent lady had a very high efteem
for it, fo fhe had an opportunity of attending it but the very Lord's day immediately
preceding her death, which happened Oct.
7, 1725, after her fon had been removed
from her almoft a year.   He had maintained her handfomely out of that very moder-
ate income, on which he fubfifted fince his
regiment had been difbanded ; and when
fhe expreffed her gratitude to him for it, he
affured her, (I think in one of the laft letters
fhe ever received from him) " that he ef-
" teemed it a great honour, that God put it
" into his power, to make (what he called) a
                                        " very

" *very fmall acknowledgment* of all her care
" for him, and efpecially of the many prayers
" fhe had offered on his account, which had
" already been remarkably anfwered, and
" the benefit of which he hoped ever to en-
" joy."

I apprehend that the Earl of Stair's regiment, to the Majority of which he was promoted
on the 20th of July, 1724, was then
quartered in Scotland ; for all the letters in
my hand, from that time to the 6th of Feb.
1726, are dated from thence, and particularly from Douglas, Stranrawen, and Air : But
I have the pleafure to find, from comparing
thefe with others of an earlier date from London and the neighboring parts, that neither
the detriment which he muft fuffer by being
fo long out of commiffion, nor the hurry of
affairs while charged with it, could prevent
or interrupt that intercourfe with heaven,
which was his daily feaft, and his daily
ftrength.

Thefe were moft eminently the happy
years of his life : For he had learned to efti-
mate his happinefs, not by the increafe of
honour, or the poffeffion of wealth, or by
what was much dearer to his generous heart
than either, the converfe of the deareft and
worthieft human friends ; but by nearnefs
to God, and by opportunities of humble
converfe

converfe with him, in the lively exercife of contemplation, praife, and prayer. Now there was no period of his life, in which he was more eminently favoured with thefe ; nor do I find any of his letters fo overflow_ ing with tranfports of holy joy, as thofe which were dated during this time. There are indeed in fome of them fuch very fub_ lime paffages, that I have been dubious whether I fhould communicate them to the public or not ; left I fhould adminifter mat_ ter of profane ridicule to fome, who look upon all the elevations of devotion as a con_ temptible enthufiafm. And it has alfo giv_ en me fome apprehenfions, left it fhould dif_ courage fome pious Chriftians, who after having fpent feveral years in the fervice of God, and in humble obedience to the pre_ cepts of his gofpel, may not have attained to any fuch heights as thefe. But on the whole, I cannot fatisfy myfelf to fupprefs them ; not only as I number fome of them, confidered in a devotional view, among the moft extraordinary pieces of the kind I have ever met with ; but as fome of the moft ex_ cellent and judicious perfons I any where know, to whom I have read them, have af_ fured me, that they felt their hearts in an unufual manner impreffed, quickened, and edified by them.

I will

I will therefore draw back the veil, and shew my much honoured friend in his moft fecret receffes, that the world may fee what thofe fprings were, from whence iffued that clear, permanent, and living ftream of wifdom, piety, and virtue, which fo apparently ran through all that part of his life which was open to public obfervation. It is not to be imagined, that letters written in the intimacy of Chriftian friendfhip, fome of them with the moft apparent marks of hafte, and amidft a variety of important public cares, fhould be adorned with any ftudied elegance of expreffion, about which the greatnefs of his foul would not allow him to be at any time very folicitous ; for he generally (fo far as I could obferve) wrote as faft as his pen could move, which happily, both for him and his many friends, was very freely. Yet here the grandeur of his fubject has fometimes clothed his ideas with a language more elevated, than is ordinarily to be expected in an epiftolary correfpondence. The proud fcorners, who may deride fentiments and enjoyments like thofe which this truly great man fo experimentally and pathetically defcribes, I pity from my heart ; and grieve to think how unfit they muft be for the Hallelujahs of heaven, who pour contempt upon the neareft approaches to
                                        them :

them : Nor fhall I think it any misfortune to fhare with fo excellent a perfon in their profane derifion. It will be infinitely more than an equivalent for all that fuch ignorance and petulency can think and fay, if I may convince fome who are as yet ftrangers to religion, how real, and how noble its delights are ; if I may engage my pious readers to glorify God for fo illuftrious an inftance of his grace ; and finally, if I may quicken them, and above all may roufe my own too indulgent fpirit, to follow with lefs unequal fteps an example, to the fublimity of which I fear few of us fhall after all be able fully to attain. And that we may not be too much difcouraged under the deficiency, let it be recollected, that few have the advantage of a temper naturally fo warm ; few have an equal command of retirement ; and perhaps hardly any one, who thinks himfelf moft indebted to the riches and freedom of divine grace, can trace interpofitions of it, in all refpects equally aftonifhing.

The firft of thefe extraordinary letters which have fallen into my hand, is dated near three years after his converfion, and addreffed to a lady of quality. I believe it is the firft the Major ever wrote, fo immediately on the fubject of his religious confolations and converfe with God in devout

H   retirement.

retirement.   For I well remember, that he
once told me, he was so much afraid that
something of spiritual pride should mingle
itself with the relation of such kind of experiences, that he concealed them a long time.
But obferving with how much freedom the
facred writers open all the moft fecret receffes of their hearts, efpecially in the Pfalms,
his confcience began to be burdened, under
an apprehenfion, that for the honor of God,
and in order to engage the concurrent praifes
of fome of his people, he ought to difclofe
them.   On this he fet himfelf to reflect, who
among all his numerous acquaintance feemed at once the moft experienced Chriftian
he knew, (to whom therefore fuch things as
he had to communicate might appear folid
and credible) and who the humbleft.   He
quickly thought of the Lady Marchionefs of
Douglas in this view : And the reader may
well imagine, that it ftruck my mind very
ftrongly, to think that now, more than 24
years after it was written, Providence fhould
bring to my hands (as it has done within
thefe few days) what I affuredly believe to
be a genuine copy of that very letter ; which
I had not the leaft reafon to expect I fhould
ever have feen, when I learnt from his own
mouth, amidft the freedom of an accidental
converfation,

converſation, the occaſion and circumſtances of it.

It is dated from London, July 21, 1722, and the very firſt lines of it relate to a remarkable circumſtance, which from others of his letters I find to have happened ſeveral times.   I mean, that when he had received from any of his Chriſtian friends a few lines which particularly affected his heart, he could not ſtay till the ſtated return of his devotional hour, but immediately retired to pray for them, and to give vent to thoſe religious emotions of mind, which ſuch a correſpondence raiſed.   How invaluable was ſuch a friend! and how great reaſon have thoſe of us, who once poſſeſſed a large ſhare in his heart, and in thoſe retired and ſacred moments, to bleſs God for ſo ſingular a felicity; and to comfort ourſelves in a pleaſing hope, that we may yet reap future bleſſings, as the harveſt of thoſe petitions which he can no more repeat!

His words are theſe: " I was ſo happy as " to receive your's juſt as I arrived, and I " had no ſooner read it, but I ſhut my door, " and *ſought him whom my ſoul loveth.   I* " *ſought him, and found him; and would not* " *let him go, till he had bleſſed us all.*   It is " impoſſible to find words to expreſs what I " obtained; but I ſuppoſe it was ſomething
" like

" like that which the difciples got, as they
" were going to Emmaus, when they faid,
" *Did not our hearts burn within us, &c.* or
" rather like what Paul felt, when he *could*
" *not tell whether he was in the body or out of*
" *it.*" He then mentions his dread of fpiritual pride, from which he earneftly prays
that God may deliver and preferve him.
" This," fays he, " would have hindered
" me from communicating thefe things, if I
" had not fuch an example before me as the
" man after God's own heart, faying, *I will*
" *declare what God hath done for my foul ;*
" and elfewhere, *The humble fhall hear there-*
" *of, and be glad :* Now I am well fatisfied,
" that your Ladyfhip is of that number."
He then adds, " I had no fooner finifhed
" this exercife," that is, of prayer above
mentioned, " but I fat down to admire the
" goodnefs of my God, that he would vouch-
" fafe to influence by his free fpirit fo un-
" deferving a wretch as I, and to make me
" thus to *mount up with eagles wings.* And
" here I was loft again, and got into an
" ocean, where I could find neither bound
" nor bottom ; but was obliged to cry out
" with the Apoftle, *O the breadth, the length,*
" *the depth, the height, of the love of Chrift,*
" *which paffeth knowledge !* But if I give way
" to this ftrain, I fhall never have done.
                              " That

" That *the God of hope may fill you with all*
" *joy and peace in believing,* that you may
" *abound in hope through the power of the*
" *Holy Ghoſt,* ſhall always be the prayer of
" him, who is, with the greateſt ſincerity
" and reſpect, your Ladyſhip's, &c."

Another paſſage to the ſame purpoſe I
find in a memorandum, which he ſeems to
have written for his own uſe, dated Monday,
March 11, which, I perceive from many
concurrent circumſtances, muſt have been
in the year 1722-3. " This day," ſays he,
" having been to viſit Mrs. G. at Hamp-
" ſtead, I came home about two, and read a
" ſermon on thoſe words, Pſalm cxxx. 4.
" *But there is forgiveneſs with thee, that thou*
" *mayeſt be feared* : About the latter end of
" which, there is a deſcription of the miſer-
" able condition of thoſe that are ſlighters of
" pardoning grace.   From a ſenſe of the
" great obligations I lay under to the Al-
" mighty God, who hath made me to differ
" from ſuch, from what I was, and from the
" reſt of my companions, I knelt down to
" praiſe his holy name : And I know not,
" that in my life time I ever lay lower in the
" duſt, never having had a fuller view of my
" own unworthineſs.   I never pleaded more
" ſtrongly the merits and interceſſion of
" him, who I know is worthy ; never vowed

" more fincerely to be the Lord's, and to
" accept of Chrift as he is offered in the
" gofpel, as my king, prieft, and prophet;
" never had fo ftrong a defire to depart, that
" I might fin no more ; but—*my grace is*
" *fufficient*—curbed that defire. I never
" pleaded with greater fervency for the com-
" forter, which our bleffed Lord hath prom-
" ifed, *fhall abide with us forever.* For all
" which I defire to afcribe glory, &c. *to him*
" *that fitteth on the throne, and to the lamb.''*

There are feveral others of his papers,
which fpeak much the fame language ;
which, had he kept a diary, would, I doubt
not, have filled many fheets. I believe, my
devout readers would not foon be weary of
reading extracts of this kind : But that I
may not exceed in this part of my narrative,
I fhall mention only two more, each of them
dated fome years after ; that is, one from
Douglas, April 1, 1725 ; and the other from
Stranrawen, the 25th of May following.

The former of thefe relates to the frame
of his fpirit on a journey. On the mention
of which I cannot but recollect, how often
I have heard him fay, that fome of the moft
delightful days of his life were days in which
he travelled alone, (that is, with only a fervant at a diftance) when he could, efpecially
in roads not much frequented, indulge him-
                                             felf

felf in the pleafures of prayer and praife.
In the exercife of which laft, he was greatly
affifted by feveral Pfalms and Hymns, which
he had treafured up in his memory, and
which he ufed not only to repeat aloud, but
fometimes to fing.   In reference to this I remember the following paffage, in a letter
which he wrote to me many years after,
when on mentioning my ever dear and honoured friend, the Rev. Dr. Watts, he fays,
" How often in finging fome of his Pfalms,
" Hymns, or Lyricks, on horfeback, and
" elfewhere, has the evil fpirit been made to
" flee !

 " Whene'er my heart in tune was found,
 " Like David's harp of folemn found !"

Such was the firft of April above mentioned, in the evening of which he writes
thus to an intimate fiiend : " What would
" I have given this day, upon the road, for
" paper, pen, and ink, when *the fpirit of the*
" *Moft High refted upon me !* Oh for the pen
" of a ready writer, and the tongue of an
" angel, to declare what God hath done this
" day for my foul ! But in fhort it is in vain
" to attempt it : All that I am able to fay,
" is only this, that my foul has been for fome
" hours joining with the bleffed fpirits a-
" bove, in giving *glory, and honour, and*
        " *praife,*

" *praife, unto him that fitteth upon the throne,*
" *and to the lamb, for ever and ever.* My
" praifes began from a renewed view of him,
" *whom I faw pierced for my tranfgreffions.*
" I fummoned the whole hierarchy of heav‑
" en to join with me ; and I am perfuaded
" they all echoed back praife to the Moft
" High. Yea, one would have thought the
" very larks joined me with emulation.
" Sure then I need not make ufe of many
" words, to perfuade *you* that are *his faints,*
" to join me in blefling and praifing his holy
" name." He concludes, " May the blefl‑
" ing of the God of Jacob reft upon you
" all ! Adieu. Written in great hafte, late,
" and weary."

Scarce can I here refrain from breaking
out into more copious reflections on the ex‑
quifite pleafures of true religion, when rifen
to fuch eminent degrees ; which can thus
feaft the foul in its folitude, and refrefh it
on journeys ; and bring down fo much of
heaven to earth, as this delightful letter ex‑
prefles. But the remark is fo obvious, that
I will not enlarge upon it ; but proceed to
the other letter above mentioned, which was
written the next month, on the Tuefday af‑
ter a facrament day.

He mentions the pleafure with which he
had attended a preparation fermon the Sat‑
urday

urday before ; and then he adds, " I took a
" walk upon the mountains that are over
" againſt Ireland ; and I perſuade myſelf,
" that were I capable of giving you a de-
" ſcription of what paſſed there, you would
" agree, that I had much better reaſon to
" remember my God from the hills of Port
" Patrick, than David from the *land of Jor-*
" *dan, and of the Hermonites, from the hill of*
" *Mizar.*" I ſuppoſe he means in reference to the clearer diſcoveries of the goſpel
with which we are favoured. " In ſhort,"
ſays he immediately afterwards, in that ſcripture phraſe which was become ſo familiar to
him, " I *wreſtled* ſome hours *with the Angel*
" *of the covenant,* and *made ſupplications to*
" *him,* with floods of tears and cries, until I
" had almoſt expired : But he ſtrengthened
" me ſo, that like Jacob I had power with
" God, and *prevailed.* This," adds he, " is
" but a very faint deſcription : You will be
" more able to judge of it by what you have
" felt yourſelf upon the like occaſions. Af-
" ter ſuch preparatory work, I need not tell
" you, how bleſſed the ſolemn ordinance of
" the Lord's ſupper proved to me ; I hope
" it was ſo to many. You may believe, I
" ſhould have been exceeding glad, if my
" gracious Lord had ordered it ſo, that I
" might have made you a viſit as I propoſed :

" ed : But I am now glad it was ordered
" otherwife, fince he hath caufed *fo much of*
" *his goodnefs to pafs before me.* Were I to
" give you an account of the many favours
" my God hath loaded me with, fince I
" parted from you, I muft have taken up
" many days in nothing but writing. I hope
" you will join with me in praifes for all the
" goodnefs he has fhewn to your unworthy
" brother in the Lord."

Such were the ardours and elevations of
his foul : But while I record thefe memorials of them, I am very fenfible, there are
many who will be inclined to cenfure them
as the flights of enthufiafm ; for which reafon I muft beg leave to add a remark or two·
on the occafion, which will be illuftrated by
feveral other extracts, which I fhall introduce into the fequel of thefe memoirs. The
one is, that he never pretends, in any of the
paffages cited above, or elfewhere, to have ·
received any immediate revelations from
God, which fhould raife him above the ordinary methods of inftruction, or difcover
any thing to him, whether of doctrines or
facts. No man was farther from pretending
to predict future events, except it were from
the moral prognoftications of caufes naturally tending to produce them ; in tracing of
which he had indeed an admirable fagacity,

as

as I have feen in fome very remarkable inftances.   Neither was he at all inclinable to
govern himfelf by fecret impulfes upon his
mind, leading him to things for which he
could affign no reafon but the impulfe itfelf.   Had he ventured, in a prefumption on
fuch fecret agitations of mind, to teach, or
to do any thing, not warranted by the dictates of found fenfe and the word of God, I
fhould readily have acknowledged him an
enthufiaft ; unlefs he could have produced
fome other evidence than his own perfuafion, to have fupported the authority of
them.   But thefe ardent expreffions, which
fome may call enthufiafm, feem only to evidence a heart deeply affected with a fenfe of
the divine prefence and perfections, and of
that love which paffeth knowledge ; efpecially, as manifefted in our redemption by
the fon of God, which did indeed inflame
his whole foul.   And he thought he might
reafonably afcribe the ftrong impreffions, to
which men are generally fuch ftrangers, and
of which he had long been entirely defti-
tute, to the agency or influence of the fpirit
of God upon his heart ; and that, in proportion to the degree in which he felt
them, he might properly fay, God was
prefent with him, and he converfed with
God.

God.*   Now when we confider the fcrip-
tural phrafes, of *walking with God*, of *having
communion with the Father and his Son Jefus
Chrift*, of *Chrift's coming to them that open
the door of their hearts to him, and fupping
with them*, of *God's fhedding abroad his love
in the heart by his fpirit*, of *his coming with
Jefus Chrift, and making his abode with any
man that loves him*, of *his meeting him that
worketh righteoufnefs*, of *his making us glad
by the light of his countenance*, and a variety
of other equivalent expreffions; I believe
we fhall fee reafon to judge much more fa-
vourably

---

* The ingenious and pious Mr. Grove, (who I think
was as little fufpected of running into *enthufiaftical extremes* as moft divines I could name) has a noble paffage
to this purpofe, in the fixth volume of his Pofthumous
Works, p. 40, 41, which refpect to the memory of both
thefe excellent perfons, inclines me to infert here.—
" How often are good thoughts fuggefted," (viz. to the
pure in heart) " heavenly affections kindled and inflamed!
" How often is the Chriftian prompted to holy actions,
" drawn to his duty, reftored, quickened, perfuaded, in
" fuch a manner, that he would be unjuft to the *fpirit of
" God*, to queftion his *agency* in the whole! Yes, oh my
" foul, there is a Supreme Being, who governs the world,
" and is prefent with it, who takes up his more fpecial
" habitation in good men, and is *nigh to all who call upon
" him*, to fanctify and affift them! Haft thou not felt him,
" oh my foul, *like another foul*, actuating thy faculties, ex-
" alting thy views, purifying thy paffions, exciting thy
" graces, and begetting in thee an abhorrence of fin, and
" a love of holinefs? And is not all this an argument of
" his prefence, as truly as if thou *didft fee him?*"

vourably of such expressions as those now in question, than persons who are themselves strangers to elevated devotion, and perhaps converse but little with their Bible, are inclined to do; especially if they have, as many such persons have, a temper that inclines them to cavil and find fault. And I must farther observe, that amidst all those freedoms, with which this eminent Christian opens his devout heart to the most intimate of his friends, he still speaks with profound awe and reverence of his heavenly father, and his saviour, and maintains (after the example of the sacred writers themselves) a kind of dignity in his expressions, suitable to such a subject; without any of that fond familiarity of language, and degrading meanness of phrase, by which it is, especially of late, grown fashionable among some, (who nevertheless I believe mean well) to express their love and their humility.

On the whole; if habitual love to God, firm faith in the Lord Jesus Christ, a steady dependence on the divine promises, a full persuasion of the wisdom and goodness of all the dispensations of providence, a high esteem for the blessings of the heavenly world, and a sincere contempt for the vanities of this, can properly be called enthusiasm; then was Colonel Gardiner indeed

I   one

one of the greateſt enthuſiaſts our age has produced ; and in proportion to the degree in which he was ſo, I muſt eſteem him one of the wiſeſt and happieſt of mankind. Nor do I fear to tell the world, that it is the deſign of my writing theſe memoirs, and of every thing elſe that I undertake in life, to ſpread this glorious and bleſſed enthuſiaſm ; which I know to be the anticipation of heaven, as well as the moſt certain way to it.

But leſt any ſhould poſſibly imagine, that allowing the experiences which have been deſcribed above, to have been ever ſo ſolid and important, yet there may be ſome appearance of boaſting in ſo free a communication of them ; I muſt add to what I have hinted in reference to this above, that I find in many of the papers before me very genuine expreſſions of the deepeſt humility and ſelf abaſement ; which indeed ſuch holy converſe with God in prayer and praiſe, does above all things in the world tend to inſpire and promote. Thus in one of his letters he ſays, " I am but as a beaſt before " him." In another he calls himſelf " a " miſerable hell deſerving ſinner :" And in another he cies out, " Oh, how good a maſ- " ter do I ſerve ! but alas, how ungrateful " am I ! What can be ſo aſtoniſhing as the

" love

" love of Chrift to us, unlefs it be the cold-
" nefs of our finful hearts towards fuch a
" Saviour ?" With many other claufes of
the like nature, which 1 fhall not fet myfelf
more particularly to trace, through the variety of letters in which they occur.

It is a farther inftance of this unfeigned
humility, that. when (as his lady with her
ufual propriety of language exprefles it, in
one of her letters to me concerning him)
" thefe divine joys and confolations were
" not his daily allowance," he with equal
freedom, in the confidence of Chriftian
friendfhip, acknowledges and laments it.
Thus in the firft letter I had the honour of
receiving from him, dated from Leicefter,
July 9, 1739, when he had been mentioning
the bleffing with which it had pleafed God
to attend my laft addrefs to him, and the in-
influence it had upon his mind, he adds,
" Much do I ftand in need of every help, to
" awaken me out of that fpiritual deadnefs,
" which feizes me fo often.   Once indeed it
" was quite otherwife with me, and that for
" many years :

   " Firm was my health, my day was bright,
   " And I prefum'd 'twould ne'er be night :
   " Fondly I faid within my heart,
   " Pleafure and peace fhall ne'er depart.

                              " But

" But I forgot, thine arm was ftrong,
" Which made my mountain ftand fo long;
" Soon as thy face began to hide,
" My health was gone, my comforts died."

" And here," adds he, " lies my fin, and my folly."

I mention this, that the whole matter may be feen juft as it was, and that other Chriftians may not be difcouraged, if they feel fome a- batement of that fervour, and of thofe holy joys, which they may have experienced dur- ing fome of the firft months or years of their fpiritual life. But with relation to the Col- onel, I have great reafon to believe, that thefe which he laments as his days of fpir- itual deadnefs were not unanimated; and that quickly after the date of this letter, and efpecially nearer the clofe of his life, he had farther revivings, as the joyful anticipation of thofe better things in referve, which were then nearly approaching. And thus Mr. Spears, in the letter I mentioned above, tells us he related the matter to him; (for he ftudies as much as poffible to retain the Colonel's own words:) " However," fays he, " after that happy period of fenfible " communion, though my joys and enlarge- " ments were not fo overflowing and fenfi- " ble, yet I have had habitual real commun- " ion with God from that day to this;" the

latter

latter end of the year 1743; " and I know
" myfelf, and all that know me fee, that
" through the grace of God, to which I af-
" cribe all, my converfation has been be-
" coming the gofpel ; and let me die, when-
" ever it fhall pleafe God, or wherever it
" fhall be, I am fure I fhall go to the man-
" fions of eternal glory," &c.   And this is
perfectly agreeable to the manner in which
he ufed to fpeak to me on this head, which
we have talked over frequently and largely.

In this connection I hope my reader will
forgive my inferting a little ftory, which I
received from a very worthy minifter in
Scotland, and which I fhall give in his own
words : " In this period," meaning that
which followed the firft feven years after his
converfion, " when his complaint of com-
" parative deadnefs and languor in religion
" began, he had a dream ; which, though
" he had no turn at all for taking notice of
" dreams, yet made a very ftrong impreffion
" upon his mind.   He imagined that he
" faw his bleffed Redeemer on earth, and
" that he was following him through a large
" field, *following him whom his foul loved,*
" but much troubled, becaufe he thought
" his bleffed Lord did not fpeak to him ;
" till he came up to the gate of a burying
" place, when turning about he fmiled upon

I 2   " him,

" him, in fuch a manner as filled his foul
" with the moſt raviſhing joy ; and on after
" reflection animated his faith, in believing
" that whatfoever ſtorms and darkneſs he
" might meet with in the way, at the hour
" of death his glorious Redeemer would
" lift up upon him the light of his life giv-
" ing countenance." My correſpondent
adds a circumſtance, for which he makes
ſome apology, as what may ſeem whimſical,
and yet made ſome impreſſion on himſelf;
" that there was a remarkable reſemblance
" in the field in which this brave man met
" death, and that he had repreſented to him
" in the dream." I did not fully under-
ſtand this at firſt ; but a paſſage in that letter from Mr. Spears, which I have mentioned more than once, has cleared it.
" Now obſerve, Sir, this ſeems to be a liter-
" al deſcription of the place where this
" Chriſtian Hero ended his ſorrows and
" conflicts, and from which he entered tri-
" umphantly *into the joys of his Lord.* For
" after he fell in the battle, fighting glori-
" ouſly for his King and the cauſe of his
" God, his wounded body, while life was
" yet remaining, was carried from the field
" of battle by the eaſt ſide of his own inclo-
" ſure, till he came to the church yard of
" Tranet, and was brought to the miniſter's
                                    " houſe,

" houfe, where he foon after breathed out
" his foul into the hands of his Lord, and
" was conducted to his prefence, where there
" is *fulnefs of joy*, without any cloud of in-
" terruption forever."

I well know, that in dreams there are di-
verfe vanities, and readily acknowledge, that
nothing certain could be inferred from this:
Yet it feems at leaft to fhew, which way the
imagination was working, even in fleep; and
I cannot think it unworthy of a wife and
good man, fometimes to reflect with com-
placency on any images, which paffing
through his mind even in that ftate, may
tend either to exprefs, or to quicken, his
love to the great Saviour.   Thofe eminently pious divines of the church of England,
Bifhop Bull, and Bifhop Kenn, do both intimate it as their opinion, that it may be a
part of the fervice of miniftering angels to
fuggeft devout dreams :* And I know, that
the

___

* Bifhop Bull has thefe remarkable words: " Although
" I am no doater on dreams, yet I verily believe, that
" fome dreams are monitory, above the power of fancy,
" and impreffed upon us by fome fuperior influence.   For
" of fuch dreams we have plain and undeniable inftances
" in hiftory, both facred and profane, and in our own age
" and obfervation.   Nor fhall I fo value the laughter of
" fceptics, and the fcoffs of the Epicureans, as to be afham-
" ed to profefs, that I myfelf have had fome convincing
" experiments of fuch impreffions."
Bifh. Bull's Serm. vol. II. p. 489, 490.

the worthy perfon of whom I fpeak, was
well acquainted with that midnight hymn of
the latter of thofe excellent writers, which
has thefe lines :

    " Lord, left the tempter me furprife,
    " Watch over thine own facrifice !
    " All loofe, all idle thoughts caft out,
    " And make my very dreams devout !"

Nor would it be difficult to produce other
paffages much to the fame pnrpofe,* if it
would not be deemed too great a digreffion
from our fubject, and too laboured a vindi-
cation of a little incident, of very fmall importance, when compared with moft of thofe
which make up this narrative.

I meet not with any other remarkable e-
vent relating to Major Gardiner, which can
                      properly

* If I miftake not, the fame Bifhop Kenn is the author
of a midnight hymn, concluding with thefe words :
    " May my etherial guardian kindly fpread
    " His wings, and from the tempter fcreen my head ;
    " Grant of celeftial light fome piercing beams,
    " To blefs my fleep, and fanctify my dreams !"

As he certainly was of thofe exactly parallel lines—
    " Oh may my guardian while I fleep,
    " Clofe to my bed his vigils keep ;
    " His love angelical inftil,
    " Stop all the avenues of ill !
    " May he celeftial joys rehearfe,
    " And thought to thought with me cenverfe !"

properly be introduced here, till the year
1726 ; when, on the 11th of July, he was
married to the Right Hon. the Lady Frances
Erſkine, daughter to the late Earl of Bu-
chan, by whom he had thirteen children,
five only of which ſurvived their father, two
ſons and three daughters : Whom I cannot
mention without the moſt fervent prayers to
God for them, that they may always behave
worthy the honour of being deſcended from
ſuch parents ; and that the God of their father, and of their mother, may make them
perpetually the care of his providence, and
yet more eminently happy in the conſtant
and abundant influences of his grace !

As her ladyſhip is ſtill living, (and for the
ſake of her dear offspring, and numerous
friends, may ſhe long be ſpared) I ſhall not
here indulge myſelf in ſaying any thing of
her, except it be, that the Colonel aſſured
me, when he had been happy in this intimate
relation to her more than fourteen years,
that the greateſt imperfection he knew in her
character was, " that ſhe valued and loved
" him, much more than he deſerved." And
little did he think, in the ſimplicity of heart
with which he ſpoke this, how high an en-
comium he was making upon her, and how
laſting an honour ſuch a teſtimony muſt
leave

leave upon her name, as long as the memory of it shall continue.

As I do not intend in these memoirs a laboured essay on the character of Colonel Gardiner, digested under the various virtues and graces which Christianity requires, (which would, I think, be a little too formal for a work of this kind, and would give it such an air of panegyric, as would neither suit my design, nor be at all likely to render it more useful;) I shall now mention what I have either observed in him, or heard concerning him, with regard to those domestic relations which commenced about this time, or quickly after. And here my reader will easily conclude, that the resolution of Joshua was from the first adopted and declared, *As for me, and my house, we will serve the Lord.* It will naturally be supposed, that as soon as he had a house, he erected an altar in it ; that the word of God was read there, and prayers and praises were constantly offered. These were not to be omitted, on account of any guest ; for he esteemed it a part of due respect to those that remained under his roof, to take it for granted, they would look upon it as a very bad compliment, to imagine they would have been obliged, by neglecting the duties of religion on their account. As his family increased, he had a

minister

minifter ftatedly refident in his houfe, who
both difcharged the office of a tutor to his
children, and of a chaplain ; and who was
always treated with a becoming kindnefs
and refpect.   But in his abfence, the Colonel himfelf led the devotions of the family ;
and they were happy, who had an opportunity of knowing, with how much folèmnity,
fervour, and propriety, he did it.

He was conftant in attendance upon publick worfhip, in which an exemplary care
was taken, that the children and fervants
might accompany the heads of the family.
And how he would have refented the non
attendance of any member of it, may eafily
be conjectured, from a free, but lively paffage, in a letter to one of his intimate friends,
on an occafion which it is not material to
mention : " Oh, Sir, had a child of yours
" under my roof, but once neglected the
" publick worfhip of God, when he was able
" to attend it, I fhould have been ready to
" conclude he had been diftracted, and
" fhould have thought of fhaving his head,
" and confining him in a dark room."

He always treated his Lady with a manly
tendernefs, giving her the moft natural evidences of a cordial habitual efteem, and expreffing a moft affectionate fympathy with
her, under the infirmities of a very delicate
constitution,

conftitution, much broken, at leaft towards the latter years of their marriage, in confequence of fo frequent pregnancy. He had at all times a moft faithful care of all her interefts, and efpecially thofe relating to the ftate of religion in her mind. His converfation and his letters concurred to cherifh thofe fublime ideas which Chriftanity fuggefts ; to promote our fubmiffion to the will of God, to teach us to center our happinefs in the great Author of our being, and to live by faith in the invifible world. Thefe, no doubt, were frequently the fubjects of mutual difcourfe : And many letters, which her Ladyfhip has had the goodnefs to communicate to me, are moft convincing evidences of the degree in which this noble and moft friendly care filled his mind, in the days of their feparation ; days, which fo entire a mutual affection muft have rendered exceeding painful, had they not been fupported by fuch exalted fentiments of piety, and fweetened by daily communion with an ever prefent and ever gracious God.

The neceffity of being fo many months together diftant from his family, hindered him from many of thofe condefcending labours in cultivating the minds of his children in early life, which to a foul fo benevolent, fo wife, and fo zealous, would undoubtedly

doubtedly have afforded a very exquifite pleafure.   The care of his worthy confort, who well knew that it is one of the brighteft parts of a mother's charaƇer, and one of the moft important views in which the fex can be confidered, made him the eafier under fuch a circumftance : But when he was with them, he failed not to inftruƇ and admonifh them ; and the conftant deep fenfe with which he fpoke of divine things, and the real unaffeƇed indifference which he always fhewed for what this vain world is moft ready to admire, were excellent leffons of daily wifdom, which I hope they will recol-leƇ with advantage in every future fcene of life.   And I have feen fuch hints in his let-ters relating to them, as plainly fhew with how great a weight they lay on his mind, and how highly he defired above all things, that they might be the faithful difciples of Chrift ; and acquainted betimes with the unequalled pleafures and bleffings of relig-ion.   He thought an excefs of delicacy, and of indulgence, one of the moft dangerous faults in education, by which he every where faw great numbers of young people undone : yet he was folicitous to guard againft a fe-verity, which might terrify or difcourage ; and though he endeavoured to take all pru-dent precautions to prevent the commiffion

K   of

of faults, yet, when they had been committed, and there feemed to be a fenfe of them, he was always ready to make the moft candid allowances for the thoughtleffnefs of unripened years, and tenderly to cherifh every purpofe of a more proper conduct for the time to come.

It was eafy to perceive, that the openings of genius in the young branches of his family gave him great delight, and that he had a fecret ambition to fee them excel in what they undertook. Yet he was greatly cautious over his heart, left it fhould be too fondly attached to them; and as he was one of the moft eminent proficients I ever knew in the bleffed fcience of refignation to the divine will, fo there was no effect of that refignation which appeared to me more admirable than what related to the life of his children. An experience, which no length of time will ever efface out of my memory, has fo fenfibly taught me, how difficult it is fully to fupport the Chriftian character here, that I hope my reader will pardon me, (I am fure at leaft the heart of wounded parents will) if I dwell a little longer upon fo interefting a fubject.

When he was in Herefordfhire, in the month of July, 1734, it pleafed God to vifit his little family with the fmall pox. Five

days

days before the date of the letter I am juſt
going to mention, he had received the agree‑
able news, that there was a profpeſt of the
recovery of his fon, then under that awful
viſitation ; and he had been expreſſing his
thankfulneſs for it, in a letter which he had
fent away but a few hours before he was in‑
formed of his death, the furprize of which,
in this conneſtion, muſt naturally be very
great.   But behold (fays the reverend and
worthy perfon from whom I received the
copy) his truly filial fubmiſſion to the will
of his heavenly father, in the following lines
addreſſed to the dear partner of his afflictiom :
" Your refignation to the will of God under
" this difpenfation gives me more joy, than
" the death of the child has given me for‑
" row.   He to be fure is happy ; and we
" ſhall go to him, though he ſhall not return
" to us.   Oh that we had our latter end al‑
" ways in view !—We ſhall foon follow ;
" and oh what reafon have we to long for
" that glorious day, when we ſhall get quit
" of *this body of fin and death*, under which
" we now groan, and which renders this life
" fo wretched ! I defire to blefs God that
" —— [another of his children] is in fo
" good a way : But I have refigned her.
" We muſt not chufe for ourfelves ; and it
" is well we muſt not, for we ſhould often
make

" make a very bad choice. And therefore
" it is our wifdom, as well as our duty, to
" leave all with a gracious God ; who hath
" promifed, that *all things fhall work together*
" *for good to thofe that love him* : And *he is*
" *faithful that hath promifed*, who will in-
" fallibly perform it, if our unbelief does
" not ftand in the way."

The greateft trial of this kind that he ever
bore, was in the removal of his fecond fon,
who was one of the moft amiable and prom-
ifing children that has been known. The
dear little creature was the darling of all who
knew him ; and promifed very fair, fo far as
a child could be known by its doings, to
have been a great ornament to the family,
and blefling to the public. The fuddennefs
of the ftroke muft, no doubt, render it the
more painful ; for this beloved child was
fnatched away by an illnefs, which feized
him but about 15 hours before it carried
him off. He died in the month of October,
1733, at near fix years old. Their friends
were ready to fear, that his affectionate parents would be almoft overwhelmed with
fuch a lofs : But the happy father had fo
firm a perfuafion, that God had received the
dear little one to the felicities of the celeftial
world ; and at the fame time had fo ftrong
a fenfe of the divine goodnefs, in taking one

of

of his children, and that too, one who lay fo
near his heart, fo early to himfelf; that the
forrows of nature were quite fwallowed up
in the fublime joy which thefe confiderations adminiftered.   When he refleƈted,
what human life is; how many its fnares
and temptations are; and how frequently
children, who once promifed well, are in-
fenfibly corrupted, and at length undone;
with Solomon, he *bleffed the dead already
dead, more than the living who were yet alive,*
and felt an unfpeakable pleafure in looking
after the lovely infant as fafely and delight-
fully lodged in the houfe of its heavenly father.   Yea, he affured me, that his heart was
at this time fo entirely taken up with thefe
views, that he was afraid, they who did not
thoroughly know him, might fufpeƈt that he
was deficient in the natural affeƈtions of a
parent; while thus borne above the anguifh
of them, by the views which faith adminiftered to him, and which divine grace fupported in his foul.

So much did he, on one of the moft try-
ing occafions of life, manifeft of the temper
of a glorified faint; and to fuch happy purpofes did he retain thofe leffons of fubmiffion to God, and acquiefcence in him, which
I remember he once inculcated in a letter
he wrote to a lady of quality, under the ap-

K 2   prehenfion

prehenfion of a breach in her family, with
which providence feemed to threaten her,
which I am willing to infert here, though a
little out of what might feem its moft proper
place, rather than entirely to omit it. It is
dated from London, June 16, 1722, when
fpeaking of the dangerous illnefs of a dear
relative, he has thefe words: "When my
" mind runs hither," that is, to God, as its
refuge and ftrong defence, as the connection
plainly determines it, "I think I can bear
" any thing, the lofs of all, the lofs of health,
" of relations on whom I depend, and whom
" I love, all that is dear to me, without re-
" pining or murmuring. When I think,
" that God orders, difpofes, and manages all
" things, *according to the counfel of his own*
" *will ;* when I think of the extent of his
" providence, that it reaches to the minuteft
" things ; then, though a ufeful friend or
" dear relative be fnatched away by death,
" I recall myfelf, and check my thoughts
" with thefe confiderations. Is he not God,
" *from everlafting,* and *to overlafting ?* And
" has he not promifed to be a God to me ?
" A God in all his attributes, a God in all
" his perfons, a God in all his creatures and
" providences ? And fhall I dare to fay,
" What fhall I do ? Was not he the infinite
" caufe of all I met with in the creatures ?
                                        And

" And were not they the finite effects of his
" infinite love and kindnefs ? I have daily
" experienced, that the inftrument was, and
" is, what God makes it to be ; and I know,
" that this God *hath the hearts of all men in*
" *his hands,* and *the earth is the Lord's, and*
" *the fulnefs thereof.* If this earth be good
" for me, I fhall have it, for my father hath
" it all in poffeffion. If favour in the eyes
" of men be good for me, I fhall have it ;
" for the fpring of every motion in the heart
" of man is in God's hand. My dear ———
" feems now to be dying ; but God is all
" wife, and every thing is done by him for
" the beft. Shall I hold back any thing
" that is his own, when he requires it ? No,
" God forbid ! When I confider the excel-
" lency of his glorious attributes, I am fatis-
" fied with all his dealings." I perceive
by the introduction, and what follows, that
moft, if not all of this, is a quotation from
fomething written by a lady ; but whether
from fome manufcript, or a printed book;
whether exactly tranfcribed, or quoted from
memory, I cannot determine : And therefore I thought proper to infert it, as the
Major (for that was the office he bore then)
by thus interweaving it with his letter makes
it his own ; and as it feems to exprefs in a
very lively manner the principles which
                                    bore

bore him on to a conduct fo truly great and heroic, in circumftances that have overwhelmed many an heart, that could have faced danger and death with the greateft intrepidity.

I return now to confider his character in the domeftic relation of a mafter, on which I fhall not enlarge. It is however proper to remark, that as his habitual meeknefs and command of his paffions, prevented indecent fallies of ungovernable anger towards thofe in the loweft ftate of fubjection to him, (by which fome in high life do ftrangely debafe themfelves, and lofe much of their authority) fo the natural greatnefs of his mind made him folicitous to render their inferior ftations as eafy as he could ; and fo much the rather, becaufe he confidered all the children of Adam, as ftanding upon a level before their great Creator, and had alfo a deeper fenfe of the dignity and worth of every immortal foul, how meanly foever it might chance to be lodged, than moft perfons I have known. This engaged him to give his fervants frequent religious exhortations and inftructions, as I have been affured by feveral who were fo happy as to live with him under that character. One of the firft letters after he entered on his Chriftian courfe, expreffes the fame difpofition ; in
                                                    which

which with great tendernefs he recommends
a fervant, who was in a bad ftate of health, to
his mother's care, as he was well acquainted
with her condefcending temper ; mentioning at the fame time the endeavours he had
ufed, to promote his preparations for a better world, under an apprehenfion that he
would not continue long in this. And we
fhall have an affecting inftance of the prevalency of the fame difpofition, in the clofing
fcene of his life, and indeed in the laft words
he ever fpoke, which expreffed his generous
folicitude for the fafety of a faithful fervant,
who was then near him.

As it was a few years after his marriage
that he was promoted to the rank of Lieutenant Colonel, in which he continued till
he had a regiment of his own, I fhall for the
future fpeak of him by that title ; and may
not perhaps find any more proper place, in
which to mention, what it is proper for me
to fay of his behaviour and conduct as an
officer. I fhall not here enlarge on his
bravery in the field, though that was very
remarkable, as I have heard from others : I
fay, from others, for I never heard any thing
of that kind from himfelf, nor knew, till after his death, that he was prefent at almoft
every battle that was faught in Flanders,
while the illuftrious Duke of Marlborough
commanded

commanded the allied army there.   I have also been affured from feveral credible perfons, fome of whom were eye witneffes, that at the fkirmifh with the rebels at Prefton in Lancafhire, (thirty years before that engagement at the other Prefton, which deprived us of this gallant guardian of his country) he fignalized himfelf very particularly : For he headed a little body of men, I think about twelve, and fet fire to the barricado of the rebels, in the face of their whole army, while they were pouring in their fhot, by which eight of the twelve that attended him fell.   This was the laft action of the kind in which he was engaged, before the long peace which enfued : And who can exprefs how happy it was for him, and indeed for his country, of which he was ever fo generous, and in his latter years fo important a friend, that he did not fall then ; when the profanenefs which mingled itfelf with this martial rage, feemed to rend the heavens, and fhocked fome other military gentlemen, who were not themfelves remarkable for their caution in this refpect.

But I infift not on things of this nature, which the true greatnefs of his foul would hardly ever permit him to mention, unlefs when it tended to illuftrate the divine care over him in thefe extremities of danger, and
the

the grace of God in calling him from fo a-
bandoned a ftate.   It is well known, that
the character of an officer is not only to be
approved in the day of combat.   Colonel
Gardiner was truly fenfible, that every day
brought its duties along with it ; and he was
conftantly careful, that no pretence of amufement, friendfhip, or even devotion itfelf,
might prevent their being difcharged in their
feafon.   .   '

I doubt not, but the noble perfons in
whofe regiment he was Lieut. Colonel, will
always be ready to bear an honourable and
grateful teftimony to his exemplary diligence
and fidelity, in all that related to the care of
the troops over which he was fet, whether
with regard to the men or the horfes.   He
knew, that it is incumbent on thofe who
have the honour of prefiding over others,
whether in civil, ecclefiaftical, or military
offices, not to content themfelves with doing
only fo much as may preferve them from
the reproach of grofs and vifible neglect ;
but ferioufly to confider, how much they
can poffibly do, without going out of their
proper fphere, to ferve the public, by the
due infpection of thofe committed to their
care.   The duties of the clofet and of the
fanctuary, were fo adjufted, as not to inter-
' fere with thofe of the parade, or any other
                              place

place where the welfare of the regiment called him.   On the other hand, he was folicitous, not to fuffer thefe things to interfere
with religion ; a due attendance to which he
apprehended to be the fureft method of at-
taining all defirable fuccefs in every other
intereft and concern in life.   He therefore
abhorred every thing that fhould look like a
contrivance to keep his foldiers employed
about their horfes and their arms at the fea-
fons of public worfhip; (an indecency, which
I wifh there were no room to mention :) Far
from that, he ufed to have them drawn up
juft before it began, and from the parade
they went off to the houfe of God.   He
underftood the rights of confcience too well,
to impofe his own particular profeffion in
religion on others, or to ufe thofe who dif-
fered from him in the choice of its modes,
the lefs kindly or refpectfully on that account.   But as moft of his own company,
and many of the reft, chofe, when in England, to attend him to the diffenting chapel,
he ufed to march them thither in due time,
fo as to be there before the worfhip began.
And I muft do them the juftice to fay, that
fo far as I could ever difcern, when I have
feen them in large numbers before me, they
behaved with as much reverence, gravity,

and

and decorum, during the time of divine fervice, as any of their fellow worfhippers.

That his remarkable care to maintain
good difcipline among them (of which we
fhall afterwards fpeak) might be the more
effeƈtual, he made himfelf on all proper occafions acceffible to them, and expreffed a
great concern for their interefts, which being
fo genuine and fincere, naturally difcovered
itfelf in a variety of inftances.   I remember,
I had once occafion to vifit one of his dragoons, in his laft illnefs, at Harborough, and
I found the man upon the borders of eternity ; a circumftance, which, as he apprehended it himfelf, muft add fome peculiar
weight and credibility to his difcourfe.   And
he then told me, in his Colonel's abfence,
that he queftioned not, but he fhould have
everlafting reafon to blefs God on Colonel
Gardiner's account, for he had been a father
to him in all his interefts both temporal and
fpiritual.   He added, that he had vifited
him almoft every day during his illnefs,
with religious advice and inftruƈtion, as well
as taken care that he fhould want nothing
that might conduce to the recovery of his
health.   And he did not fpeak of this, as
the refult of any particular attachment to
him, but as the manner in which he was accuftomed to treat thofe under his command.

L   It

It is no wonder, that this engaged their affection to a very great degree. And I doubt not, that if he had fought the fatal battle of Prefton Pans at the head of that gallant regiment, of which he had the care for fo many years, and which is allowed by moft unexceptionable judges to be one of the fineft in the Britifh fervice, and confequently in the world, he had been fupported in a much different manner; and had found a much greater number, who would have rejoiced in an opportunity of making their own breafts a barrier in the defence of his.

It could not but greatly endear him to his foldiers, that fo far as preferments lay in his power, or were under his influence, they were diftributed according to merit; which he knew to be as much the dictate of prudence as of equity. I find by one of his letters before me, dated but a few months after his happy change, that he was folicited to improve his intereft with the Earl of Stair, in favour of one whom he judged a very worthy perfon; and that it had been fuggefted by another who recommended him, that if he fucceeded he might expect fome handfome acknowledgment. But he anfwers with fome degree of indignation, "Do you imagine I am to be bribed *to do juftice?*" For fuch it feems he efteemed it, to confer

the

the favour which was afked from him, on
one fo deferving.   Nothing can more effectually tend to humble the enemies of a ftate,
than that fuch maxims fhould univerfally
prevail in it : And if they do not prevail,
the worthieft men in an army or fleet may
be funk under repeated difcouragements,
and the bafeft exalted, to the infamy of the
public, and perhaps to its ruin.

In the midft of all the gentlenefs which
Colonel Gardiner exercifed towards his foldiers, he made it very apparent, that he
knew how to reconcile the tendernefs of a
real, faithful, and condefcending friend,
with the authority of a commander.   Perhaps hardly any thing conduced more generally to the maintaining of this authority,
than the ftrict decorum and good manners,
with which he treated even the private gentlemen of his regiment ; which has always a
great efficacy towards keeping inferiors at a
proper diftance, and forbids, in the leaft of-
fenfive manner, familiarities, which degrade
the fuperior, and enervate his influence.
The calmnefs and fteadinefs of his behaviour
on all occafions, did alfo greatly tend to the
fame purpofe.   He knew how mean a man
looks in the tranfports of paffion, and would
not ufe fo much freedom with any of his
men, as to fall into fuch tranfports before
them ;

them; well knowing, that perfons in the loweft rank of life, are aware how unfit they are to govern others, who cannot govern themfelves. He was alfo fenfible, how neceffary it is in all who prefide over others, and efpecially in military officers, to check irregularities, when they firft begin to appear: And that he might be able to do it, he kept a ftrict infpection over his foldiers; in which view it was obferved, that as he generally chofe to refide among them as much as he could, (though in circumftances which fometimes occafioned him to deny himfelf in fome interefts which were very dear to him) fo when they were around him, he feldom ftaid long in a place; but was frequently walking the ftreets, and looking into their quarters and ftables, as well as reviewing and exercifing them himfelf. It has often been obferved, that the regiment of which he was fo many years Lieutenant Colonel, was one of the moft regular and orderly regiments in the public fervice; fo that perhaps none of our dragoons were more welcome than they, to the towns where their character was known. Yet no fuch bodies of men are fo blamelefs in their conduct, but fomething will be found, efpecially among fuch confiderable numbers, worthy of cenfure, and fometimes of punifhment.

This

This Colonel Gardiner knew how to inflict with a becoming refolution, and with all the feverity which he judged neceffary : A feverity the more awful and impreffing, as it was always attended with meeknefs ; for he well knew, that when things are done in a paffion, it feems only an accidental circumftance that they are acts of juftice, and that fuch indecencies greatly obftruct the ends of punifhment, both as it relates to reforming offenders, and to deterring others from an imitation of their faults.

One inftance of his conduct, which happened at Leicefter, and was related by the perfon chiefly concerned, to a worthy friend from whom I had it, I cannot forbear inferting. While part of the regiment was encamped in the neighbourhood of that place, the Colonel went incognito to the camp in the middle of the night ; for he fometimes lodged at his quarters in the town. One of the centinels then on duty had abandoned his poft, and on being feized broke out into fome oaths, and profane execrations againft thofe that difcovered him, a crime of which the Colonel had the greateft abhorrence, and on which he never failed to animadvert. The man afterwards appeared much afhamed and concerned for what he had done. But the Colonel ordered him to be brought

early

early the next morning to his own quarters, where he had prepared a piquet, on which he appointed him a private fort of penance: and while he was put upon it, he difcourfed with him ferioufly and tenderly upon the evils and aggravations of his fault; admonifhed him of the divine difpleafure, which he had incurred; and urged him to argue from the pain which he then felt, how infinitely more dreadful it muft be, to *fall into the hands of the living God*, and indeed to meet the terrors of that damnation, which he had been accuftomed impioufly to call for on himfelf and his companions. The refult of this proceeding was, that the offender accepted his punifhment, not only with fubmiffion, but with thankfulnefs. He went away with a more cordial affection for his Colonel than ever he had before; and fpoke of it fome years after to my friend, in fuch a manner, that there feemed reafon to hope, it had been inftrumental in producing not only a change in his life, but in his heart.

There cannot, I think, be a more proper place for mentioning the great reverence this excellent officer always expreffed for the name of the bleffed God, and the zeal with which he endeavoured to fupprefs, and if poffible to extirpate, that deteftable fin of

fwearing

fwearing and curfing, which is every where
fo common, and efpecially among our military men.　He often declared his fentiments
with refpect to this enormity, at the head of
his regiment ; and urged his Captains, and
their fubalterns, to take the greateft care,
that they did not give the fanction of their
example, to that which by their office they
were obliged to punifh in others.　And indeed his zeal on thefe occafions wrought in
a very active, and fometimes in a remarkably
fuccefsful manner, not only among his e-
quals, but fometimes among his fuperiors
too.　An inftance of this in Flanders, I fhall
have an opportunity hereafter to produce ;
at prefent I fhall only mention his conduct
in Scotland a little before his death, as I
have it from a very valuable young minifter
of that country, on whofe teftimony I can
thoroughly depend ; and I wifh it may excite many to imitation.

The commanding officer of the King's
forces then about Edinburgh, with the other
Colonels, and feveral other gentlemen of
rank in their refpective regiments, favoured
him with their company at Bankton, and
took a dinner with him.　He too well fore-
faw what might happen, amidft fuch a variety of tempers and characters : And fearing,
left his confcience might have been enfnared
by

by a finful filence, or that on the other hand
he might feem to pafs the bounds of decen_
cy, and infringe upon the laws of hofpitali_
ty, by animadverting on guefts fo juftly en-
titled to his regard ; he happily determined
on the following method of avoiding each of
thefe difficulties.   As foon as they were
come together, he addreffed them with a
great deal of refpect, and yet at the fame
time with à very frank and determined air ;
and told them, that he had the honour in
that diftrict to be a juftice of the peace, and
confequently that he was fworn to put the
laws in execution, and among the reft thofe
againft fwearing : That he could not exe-
cute them upon others with any confidence,
or by any means approve himfelf as a man
of impartiality and integrity to his own
heart, if he fuffered them to be broken in his
prefence by perfons of any rank whatfoever :
And that therefore he entreated all the gen_
tlemen who then honoured him with their
company, that they would pleafe to be upon
their guard ; and that if any oath or curfe
fhould efcape them, he hoped they would
confider his legal animadverfion upon it,
as a regard to the duties of his office and the
dictates of his confcience, and not as owing
to any want of deference to them.   The
commanding officer immediately fupported
him

him in this declaration, as entirely becoming the ſtation in which he was, aſſuring him, that he would be ready to pay the penalty, if he inadvertently tranſgreſſed ; and when Colonel Gardiner on any occaſion ſtepped out of the room, he himſelf undertook to be the guardian of the law in his abſence ; and as one of the inferior officers offended during this time, he informed the Colonel, ſo that the fine was exacted, and given to the poor,* with the univerſal approbation of the company.   The ſtory ſpread in the neighborhood, and was perhaps applauded highly by many, who wanted the courage to *go and do likewiſe.*   But it may be ſaid of the worthy perſon of whom I write, with the utmoſt propriety, that he feared the face of no man living, where the honour of God was concerned.   In all ſuch caſes he might be juſtly ſaid, in ſcripture phraſe, to *ſet his face like a flint*; and I aſſuredly believe, that had he been in the preſence of a ſovereign Prince, who had been guilty of this fault, his looks

at

---

* It is obſervable, that the money, which was forfeited on this account by his own officers, whom he never ſpared, or by any others of his ſoldiers, who rather choſe to pay than to ſubmit to corporal puniſhment, was by the Colonel's order laid by in a bank, till ſome of the private men fell ſick ; and then it was laid out in providing them with proper help, and accommodations in their diſtreſs.

at leaſt would have teſtified his grief and
ſurprize, if he had apprehended it unfit to
have borne his teſtimony any other way.

Lord Cadogan's regiment of dragoons,
during the years I have mentioned, while he
was Lieutenant Colonel of it, was quartered
in a great variety of places, both in England
and Scotland, from many of which I have
letters before me ; particularly from Hamilton, Air, Carliſle, Hereford, Maidenhead,
Leiceſter, Warwick, Coventry, Stamford,
Harborough, Northampton, and ſeveral
other places, eſpecially in our inland parts.
The natural conſequence was, that the Colonel, whoſe character was on many accounts
ſo very remarkable, had a very extenſive acquaintance : And I believe I may certainly
ſay, that wherever he was known by perſons
of wiſdom and worth, he was proportionably reſpected, and left behind him traces of
unaffected devotion, humility, benevolence
and zeal, for the ſupport and advancement
of religion and virtue.

The equable tenor of his mind in theſe
reſpects, is illuſtrated by his letters from ſeveral of theſe places ; and though it is but
comparatively a ſmall number of them which
I have now in my hands, yet they will afford ſome valuable extracts ; which I ſhall
therefore here lay before my reader, that he
may

may the better judge as to his real character, in particulars of which I have already
difcourfed, or which may hereafter occur.

In a letter to his lady, dated from Carlifle,
Nov. 19, 1733, when he was on his journey
to Herefoidfhire, he breathes out his grateful cheerful foul in thefe words : " I blefs
" God, I was never better in my life time ;
" and I wifh I could be fo happy, as to hear
" the fame of you ; or rather, (in other
" words) to hear that you had obtained an
" entire *truft in God*. That would infallibly
" keep you in perfect peace ; for *the God of*
" *truth* hath promifed it. Oh, how ought
" we to be longing to be with Chrift, which
" is infinitely better than any thing we can
" propofe here ! To be there, where all
" complaints fhall be forever banifhed ;
" where no mountains fhall feparate between
" God and our fouls : And I hope it will
" be fome addition to our happinefs, that
" you and I fhall be feparated no more ;
." but that as we have joined in finging the
" praifes of our glorious redeemer here, we
" fhall fing them in a much higher key,
" through an endlefs eternity ! Oh eternity,
" eternity ! What a wonderful thought is
" eternity !"

From Leicefter, Aug. 6, 1739, he writes
thus to his lady : " Yefterday I was at the
Lord's

" Lord's table, where you and the children
" were not forgotten : But how wonderfully
" was I affifted when I came home, to plead
" for you all with many tears !" And then,
fpeaking of fome intimate friends, who were
impatient (as I fuppofe by the connection)
for his return to them, he takes occafion to
obferve the neceffity "of endeavouring to
" compofe our minds, and to fay with the
" Pfalmift, *My foul, wait thou only upon God.*"
Afterwards, fpeaking of one of his children,
of whom he heard that he made a commend-
able progrefs in learning, he expreffes his
fatisfaction in it, and adds, " But how much
" greater joy would it give me, to hear that
" he was greatly advanced in the *fchool of*
" *Chrift !* Oh that our children may but be
" *wife to falvation* ; and *may grow in grace,*
" as they do in ftature !"

Thefe letters, which to fo familiar a friend,
evidently lay open the heart, and fhew the
ideas and affections which were lodged
deepeft there, are fometimes taken up with
an account of fermons he had attended, and
the impreffion they had made upon his
mind.　I fhall mention one only, as a fpecimen of many more, which was dated from a
place called Cohorn, April 15. " We had
" here a minifter from Wales, who gave us
" two excellent difcourfes on the *love of*
" *Chrift*

" *Chrift to us,* as an argument to engage *our*
" *love to him.* And indeed, next to the
" greatnefs of his love to us, methinks there
" is nothing fo aftonifhing as the coldnefs of
" our love to him. Oh that he *would fhed*
" *abroad his love upon our hearts by his holy*
" *fpirit,* that ours might be kindled into a
" flame ! May God enable you to truft in
" him, and then you will be *kept in perfect*
" *peace !*"

We have met with many traces of that
habitual gratitude to the bleffed God, as his
heavenly father and conftant friend, which
made his life probably one of the happieft
that ever was fpent on earth.   I cannot o-
mit one more, which appears to me the more
worthy of notice, as being a fhort turn in as
hafty a letter as any I remember to have
feen of his, which he wrote from Leicefter,
in June, 1739. " I am now under the deep-
" eft fenfe of the many favours the Almigh-
" ty has beftowed upon me : Surely you
" will help me to celebrate the praifes of our
" gracious God and kind benefactor." This
exuberance of grateful affection, which,
while it was almoft every hour pouring itfelf forth before God in the moft genuine
and emphatical language, felt itfelf ftill as
it were ftraitened for want of a fufficient
vent, and therefore called on others to help

M   him

him with their concurrent praifes, appears to me the moft glorious and happy ftate in which a human foul can find itfelf on this fide heaven.

Such was the temper which this excellent man appears to have carried along with him, through fuch a variety of places and circum-ftances ; and the whole of his deportment was fuitable to thefe impreffions. Strangers were agreeably ftruck with his firft appear-ance, there was fo much of the Chriftian, the well bred man, and the univerfal friend in it ; and as they came more intimately to know him, they difcovered more and more the uniformity and confiftency of his whole temper and behaviour : So that whether he made only a vifit for a few days to any place, or continued there for many weeks or months, he was always beloved and efteem-ed, and fpoken of with that honourable tef-timony from perfons of the moft different denominations and parties, which nothing but true fterling worth, (if I may be allowed the expreffion) and that in an eminent de-gree, can fecure.

Of the juftice of this teftimony, which I had fo often heard from a variety of perfons, I myfelf began to be a witnefs about the time when the laft mentioned letter was dit-ed. In this view I believe I fhall never forget

forget that happy day, June 13, 1739, when I firſt met him at Leiceſter. I remember, I happened that day to preach a lecture from Pſalm cxix. 158. *I beheld the tranſgreſſors, and was grieved, becauſe they kept not thy law.* I was large in deſcribing that mixture of indignation and grief, (ſtrongly expreſſed by the original word there) with which the good man looks on the daring tranſgreſſors of the divine law ; and in tracing the cauſes of that grief, as ariſing from a regard to the divine honour, and the intereſt of a redeemer, and a compaſſionate concern for the miſery ſuch offenders bring on themſelves, and for the miſchief they do to the world about them. I little thought how exactly I was drawing Colonel Gardiner's character under each of thoſe heads ; and I have often reflected upon it as a happy providence, which opened a much ſpeedier way than I could have expected to the breaſt of one of the moſt amiable and uſeful friends, which I ever expect to find upon earth.   We afterwards ſung a hymn, which brought over again ſome of the leading thoughts in the ſermon, and ſtruck him ſo ſtrongly, that on obtaining a copy of it, he committed it to his memory, and uſed to repeat it with ſo forcible an accent, as ſhewed how much every line expreſſed of his very ſoul.   In this view the

reader

reader will pardon my inferting it ; efpecially, as I know not when I may get time to
publifh a volume of thefe ferious, though
artlefs compofures, which I fent him in
manufcript fome years ago, and to which I
have fince made very large additions.

Arife, my tend'reft thoughts, arife,
To torrents melt my ftreaming eyes !
And thou, my heart, with anguifh feel
Thofe evils which thou canft not heal !

See human nature funk in fhame !
See fcandals pour'd on Jefu's name !
The father wounded through the fon !
The world abus'd, the foul undone !

See the fhort courfe of vain delight
Clofing in everlafting night !
In flames that no abatement know,
The briny tears forever flow.

My God, I feel the mournful fcene ;
My bowels yearn o'er dying men :
And fain my pity would reclaim,
And fnatch the fire brands from the flame.

But feeble my compaffion proves,
And can but weep, where moft it loves.
Thine own all faving arm employ,
And turn thefe drops of grief to joy !

The Colonel, immediately after the conclufion of the fervice, met me in the veftry,
and

and embraced me in the most obliging and
affectionate manner, as if there had been a
long friendship between us ; assured me that
he had for some years been intimately acquainted with my writings ; and desired
that we might concert measures for spending
some hours together, before I left the town.
I was so happy as to be able to secure an
opportunity of doing it ; and I must leave
it upon record, that I cannot recollect I was
ever equally edified by any conversation I
remember to have enjoyed. We passed that
evening and the next morning together ;
and it is impossible for me to describe the
impression which the interview left upon my
heart. I rode alone all the remainder of
the day ; and it was my unspeakable happiness that I was alone, since I could be no
longer with him ; for I can hardly conceive
what other company would not then have
been an incumbrance. The views which
he gave me even then, (for he began to re-
pose a most obliging confidence in me,
though he concealed some of the most extraordinary circumstances of the methods by
which he had been recovered to God and
happiness) with those cordial sentiments of
evangelical piety and extensive goodness,
which he poured out into my bosom with
so endearing a freedom, fired my very soul ;

and

and I hope I may truly fay, (what I wifh and pray many of my readers may alfo a-dopt for themfelves) that I *glorified God in him.* Our epiftolary correfpondence im-mediately commenced upon my return ; and though, through the multiplicity of bufinefs on both fides, it fuffered many interruptions, it was in fome degree the blefling of all the following years of my life, till he fell by thofe unreafonable and wicked men, who had it in their hearts with him to have deftroy-ed all our glory, defence and happinefs.

The firft letter I received from him was fo remarkable, that fome perfons of eminent piety, to whom I communicated it, would not be content without copying it, or mak-ing fome extracts from it. I perfuade my-felf, that my devout reader will not be dif-pleafed, that I infert the greateft part of it here ; efpecially, as it ferves to illuftrate the affectionate fenfe which he had of the di-vine goodnefs in his converfion, though more than twenty years had paffed fince that memorable event happened. Having men-tioned my ever dear and honoured friend, Dr. Ifaac Watts, on an occafion which I hinted at above, (page 99) he adds, " I have " been in pain thefe feveral years, left that " excellent perfon, *that fweet finger in our* " *Ifrael,* fhould have been called to heaven
                                        " before

" before I had an opportunity of letting him
" know how much his works have been bleff-
" ed to me, and of courſe of returning him
" my hearty thanks : For though it is owing
" to the operation of the bleſſed ſpirit, that
" any thing works effectually upon our
" hearts, yet if we are not thankful to the
" inſtrument which God is pleaſed to make
" uſe of, *whom we do ſee,* how ſhall we be
" thankful to the Almighty, *whom we have
" not ſeen ?* I deſire to bleſs God for the
" good news of his recovery, and intreat you
" to tell him, that although I cannot keep
" pace with him here, in celebrating the high
" praiſes of our glorious redeemer, which is
" the greateſt grief of my heart ; yet I am
" perſuaded, that when I join the glorious
" company above, where there will be no
" drawbacks, none will out ſing me there ;
" becauſe I ſhall not find any, that will be
" more indebted to the wonderful riches of
" divine grace than I.

> " Give me a place at thy ſaints feet,
> " Or ſome fall'n angel's vacant ſeat ;
> " I'll ſtrive to ſing as loud as they,
> " Who ſit above in brighter day.

" I know it is natural for every one, who has
" felt the almighty power which raiſed our
" glorious redeemer from the grave, to be-
" lieve

" lieve his cafe fingular : But I have made
" every one in this refpect fubmit, as foon as
" he has heard my ftory.   And if you
" feemed fo furprized at the account which
" I gave you, what will you be when you
" hear it all ?

    " Oh if I had an angel's voice,
    " And could be heard from pole to pole ;
    " I would to all the lift'ning world
    " Proclaim thy goodnefs to my foul."

He then concludes, after fome expreffions
of endearment, (which, with whatever pleafure I review them, I muft not here infert)
" If you knew what a natural averfion I
" have to writing, you would be aftonifhed
" at the length of this letter, which is, I be-
" lieve, the longeft I ever wrote.   But my
" heart warms when I write to you, which
" makes my pen move the eafier.   I hope
" it will pleafe our gracious God long to
" preferve you, a bleffed inftrument in his
" hand, of doing great good in the church
" of Chrift ; and that you may always enjoy
" a thriving foul in a healthful body, fhall
" be the continual prayer of, &c."

  As our intimacy grew, our mutual affection increafed ; and " my deareft friend,"
was the form of addrefs with which moft of
his epiftles of the laft years were begun and
                             ended.

ended. Many of them are filled up with his sentiments of those writings which I published during these years, which he read with great attention, and of which he speaks in terms which it becomes me to suppress, and to impute in a considerable degree to the kind prejudices of so endeared a friendship. He gives me repeated assurances, " that he was daily mindful of me in his prayers ;" a circumstance which I cannot recollect without the greatest thankfulness ; the loss of which I should more deeply lament, did I not hope, that the happy effect of these prayers might still continue, and might run into all my remaining days.

It might be a pleasure to me, to make several extracts from many others of his letters : But it is a pleasure which I ought to suppress, and rather to reflect with unfeigned humility, how unworthy I was of such regards from such a person, and of that divine goodness which gave me such a friend in him. I shall therefore only add two general remarks, which offer themselves from several of his letters. The one is, that there is in some of them, as our freedom increased, an agreeable vein of humour and pleasantry ; which shews how easy religion sat upon him, and how far he was from placing any part of it in a gloomy melancholy, or stiff formality.

formality. The other is, that he frequently refers to domeſtic circumſtances, ſuch as the illneſs or recovery of my children, &c. which I am ſurpriſed how a man of his extenſive and important buſineſs could ſo diſtinctly bear upon his mind. But his memory was good, and his heart was yet better; and his friendſhip was ſuch, that nothing which ſenſibly affected the heart of one whom he honoured with it, left his own but ſlightly touched. I have all imaginable reaſon to believe, that in many inſtances his prayers were not only offered for us in general terms, but varied as our particular ſituation requir-ed. Many quotations might verify this; but I decline troubling the reader with an enumeration of paſſages, in which it was only the abundance of friendly ſympathy, that gave this truly great, as well as good man, ſo cordial a concern.

After this correſpondence, carried on for the ſpace of about three years, and ſome in-terviews which we had enjoyed at different places, he came to ſpend ſome time with us at Northampton, and brought with him his lady and his two eldeſt children. I had here an opportunity of taking a much nearer view of his character, and ſurveying it in a much greater variety of lights than before; and my eſteem for him increaſed, in proportion

portion to thefe opportunities. What I
have wrote above, with refpect to his conduct in relative life, was in a great meafure
drawn from what I now faw : And I fhall
mention here fome other points in his behaviour, which particularly ftruck my mind ;
and likewife fhall touch on his fentiments on
fome topics of importance, which he freely
communicated to me, and which I remarked
on account of that wifdom and propriety
which I apprehended in them.

There was nothing more openly obferva-
ble in Colonel Gardiner, than the exemplary gravity, compofure, and reverence, with
which he attended public worfhip. Copious as he was in his fecret devotions before
he engaged in it, he always began them fo
early, as not to be retarded by them, when
he fhould refort to the houfe of God. He,
and all his foldiers who chofe to worfhip
with him, were generally there, (as I have
already hinted) before the fervice began ;
that the entrance of fo many of them at
once might not difturb the congregation already engaged in devotion, and that there
might be the better opportunity for bringing
the mind to a becoming attention, and pre-
paring it for converfe with the divine being.
While acts of worfhip were going on, whether
of prayer or finging, he always ftood up ;
                                    and

and whatever regard he might have for perfons who paffed by him at that time, though
it were to come into the fame pew, he never
paid any compliment to them : And often
has he expreffed his wonder at the indeco-
rum of breaking off our addrefs to God, to
bow to a fellow creature ; which he thought
a much greater indecency, than it would be
on a like occafion and circumftance, to interrupt an addrefs to our Prince. During
the time of preaching, his eye was commonly fixed upon the minifter, though fometimes turned round upon the auditory, where
if he obferved any to trifle, it filled him with
juft indignation. And I have known inftances, in which, upon making the remark,
he has communicated it to fome friend of the
perfons who were guilty of it, that proper
application might be made to prevent it for
the time to come.

A more devout communicant at the table
of the Lord has perhaps feldom been any
where known. Often have I had the pleafure, to fee that manly countenance foftened
to all the marks of humiliation and contri-
tion, on this occafion ; and to difcern, in
fpite of all his efforts to conceal them, ftreams
of tears flowing down from his eyes, while he
has been directing them to thofe memorials
of his redeemer's love. And fome, who
have

have converfed intimately with him after he came from that ordinance, have obferved a vifible abftraction from furrounding objects; by which there feemed reafon to imagine, that his foul was wrapped up in holy contemplation.   And I particularly remember, that when we had once fpent great part of the following Monday in riding together, he made an apology to me for being fo abfent as he feemed, by telling me, " that his heart " was flown upwards before he was aware, " to him, *whom not having feen, he loved ;**** " and that he *was rejoicing in him with fuch* " *unfpeakable joy*, that he could not hold it " down to creature converfe."

In all the offices of friendfhip he was remarkably ready, and had a moft fweet and engaging manner of performing them, which greatly heightened the obligations he conferred.   He feemed not to fet any high value upon any benefit he beftowed ; but did it without the leaft parade, as a thing which in thofe circumftances came of courfe, where he had profeffed love and refpect, which he was not over forward to do, though he treated ftrangers, and thofe who were moft his inferiors, very courteoufly, and always feemed,

* This alluded to the fubject of the fermon the day before, which was 1 Pet. i. 8.

N

ed, becaufe he in truth always was, glad of any opportunity of doing them good.

He was particularly zealous in vindicating the reputation of his friends in their abfence : And though I cannot recollect, that I had ever an opportunity of obferving this immediately, as I do not know that I ever was prefent with him when any ill was fpoken of others at all ; yet by what I have heard him fay, with relation to attempts to injure the characters of worthy and ufeful men, I have reafon to believe, that no man living was more fenfible of the bafenefs and infamy, as well as the cruelty, of fuch a conduct. He knew, and defpifed the low principles of refentment for unreafonable expectations difappointed, of perfonal attachment to men of fome croffing interefts, of envy, and of party zeal, from whence fuch a conduct often proceeds ; and was particularly offended, when he found it (as he frequently did) in perfons that fet up for the greateft patrons of liberty, virtue and candour. He looked upon the *murderers of reputation and ufefulnefs*, as fome of the vileft pefts of fociety ; and plainly fhewed on every proper occafion, that he thought it the part of a generous, benevolent, and courageous man, to exert himfelf in tracing and hunting down the flander, that the authors or abettors of

it

it might be lefs capable of doing mifchief for the future.

The moft plaufible objection that I ever heard to Colonel Gardiner's character is, that he was too much attached to fome religious principles, eftablifhed indeed in the churches both of England and Scotland, but which have of late years been much difputed, and from which, it is at leaft generally fuppofed, not a few in both have thought proper to depart ; whatever expedients they may have found to quiet their confciences, in fubfcribing thofe formularies,- in which they are plainly taught.   His zeal was efpecially apparent in oppofition to thofe doctrines, which feemed to derogate from the divine honours of the fon and fpirit of God, and from the freedom of divine grace, or the reality and neceffity of its operations in the converfion and falvation of finners.

With relation to thefe I muft obferve, that it was his moft ftedfaft perfuafion, that all thofe notions, which reprefent our bleffed redeemer and the holy fpirit as mere creatures, or which fet afide the atonement of the former, or the influences of the latter, do fap the very foundation of Chriftianity, by rejecting the moft glorious doctrines peculiar to it.   He had attentively obferved (what indeed is too obvious) the unhappy
influence

influence which the denial of thefe principles often has on the character of minifters,
and on their fuccefs, and was perfuaded,
that an attempt to fubftitute that mutilated
form of Chriftianity which remains, when
thefe effentials of it are taken away, has
proved one of the moft fuccefsful methods
which the great enemy of fouls has ever
taken in thefe latter days, to lead men by
infenfible degrees into deifm, vice, and per-
dition.   He alfo fagacioufly obferved the
artful manner in which obnoxious tenets are
often maintained and infinuated, with all
that mixture of zeal and addrefs with which
they are propagated in the world, even by
thofe who had moft folemnly profeffed to
believe, and engaged to teach the contrary :
And as he really apprehended, that the glory of God, and the falvation of fouls was
concerned, his piety and charity made him
eager and ftrenuous in oppofing what he
judged to be errors of fo pernicious a nature.
Yet I muft declare, that according to what
I have known of him, (and I believe he
opened his heart on thefe topics to me, with
as much freedom as to any man living) he
was not ready upon light fufpicions to charge
tenets which he thought fo pernicious on
any, efpecially where he faw the appearances of a good temper and life, which he
                              always

always reverenced and loved in perfons of all fentiments and profeffions. He feverely condemned caufelefs jealoufies, and evil furmifings of every kind ; and extended that charity in this refpeEt, both to clergy and laity, which good Bifhop Burnet was fo ready, according to his own account, to limit to the latter, " of believing every man good "'till he knew him to be bad, and his no_ " tions right till he knew them wrong." He could not but be very fenfible of the unhappy confequences, which may follow on attacking the charaEters of men, efpecially of thofe who are minifters of the gofpel : And if through a mixture of human frailty, from which the beft of men in the beft of their meanings and intentions are not entirely free, he has ever, in the warmth of his heart, dropped a word which might be injurious to any on that account, (which I believe very feldom happened) he would gladly retraEt it on better information ; which was perfeEtly agreeable to that honeft and generous franknefs of temper, in which I never knew any man who exceeded him.

On the whole, it was indeed his deliberate judgment, that the Arian, Socinian, and Pelagian doEtrines, were highly difhonourable to God, and dangerous to the fouls of men ; and that it was the duty of private Chrift-

N 2   ians,

ians, to be greatly on their guard againſt thoſe miniſters by whom they are entertained, leſt their *minds ſhould be corrupted from the ſimplicity that is in Chriſt.* Yet he ſincerely abhorred the thought of perſecution for conſcience ſake ; of the abſurdity and iniquity of which, in all its kinds and degrees, he had as deep and rational a conviction, as any man I could name. And indeed the generoſity of his heroic heart could hardly bear to think, that thoſe glorious truths, which he ſo cordially loved, and which he aſſuredly believed to be capable of ſuch fair ſupport, both from reaſon and the word of God, ſhould be diſgraced by methods of defence and propagation, common to the moſt impious and ridiculous falſehoods. Nor did he by any means approve of paſſionate and furious ways of vindicating the moſt vital and important doctrines of the goſpel : For he knew, that to maintain the moſt benevolent religion in the world by ſuch malevolent and infernal methods, was *deſtroying the end to accompliſh the means ;* and that it was as impoſſible, that true Chriſtianity ſhould be ſupported thus, as it is that a man ſhould long be nouriſhed by eating his own fleſh. To diſplay the genuine fruits of Chriſtianity in a good life, to be ready to plead with meekneſs and ſweetneſs for the doctrines it teaches, and to labour by every

office

office of humanity and goodnefs to gain upon them that oppofe it, were the weapons
with which this good foldier of Jefus Chrift
faithfully fought the battles of the Lord.
Thefe weapons will always be victorious in
his caufe ; and they who have recourfe to
others of a different temperature, how ftrong
foever they may feem, and how fharp foever
they may really be, will find they break in
their hands when they exert them moft fu-
rioufly, and are much more likely to wound
themfelves, than to conquer the enemies they
oppofe.

But while I am fpeaking of Colonel Gardiner's charity in this refpect, I muft not o-
mit that of another kind, which has indeed
ingroffed the name of charity much more
than it ought, excellent as it is ; I mean
almfgiving, for which he was very remarkable. I have often wondered, how he was
able to do fo many generous things this way :
But his frugality fed the fpring. He made
no pleafurable expenfe on himfelf, and was
contented with a very decent appearance in
his family, without affecting fuch an air of
grandeur, as could not have been fupported,
without facrificing to it fatisfactions far nobler, and to a temper like his, far more delightful. The lively and tender feelings of
his heart, in favour of the diftreffed and afflicted,

flicted, made it a felf indulgence to him to relieve them; and the deep conviction he had of the vain and tranfitory nature of the enjoyments of this world, together with the fublime view he had of another, engaged him to difpenfe his bounties with a very liberal hand, and even to feek out proper objects of them: And above all, his fincere and ardent love to the Lord Jefus Chrift, engaged him to feel, with a true fympathy, the concerns of his poor members. In confequence of this, he honoured feveral of his friends with commiffions for the relief of the poor; and particularly, with relation to fome under my paftoral care, he referred it to my difcretion to fupply them with what I fhould judge expedient, and frequently preffed me in his letters *to be fure not to let them want*. And where perfons ftanding in need of his charity happened, as they often did, to be perfons of remarkably religious difpofitions, it was eafy to perceive, that he not only loved, but honoured them; and really efteemed it an honour which providence conferred upon him, that he fhould be made, as it were, *the almoner of God*, for the relief of fuch.

I cannot forbear relating a little ftory here, which, when the Colonel himfelf heard it, gave him fuch exquifite pleafure, that I hope it will be acceptable to feveral of my readers.

readers.   There was in a village about three
miles from Northampton, and in a family
which of all others' near me was afterwards
moft indebted to him, (though he had never
then feen any member of it) an aged and
poor, but eminently good woman, who had
with great difficulty, in the exercife of much
faith and patience, diligence and humility,
made fhift to educate a large family of children, after the death of her hufband, without
being chargeable to the parifh ; which, as it
was quite beyond her hope, fhe often fpoke
of with great delight.   At length, when
worn out with age and infirmities, fhe lay
upon her dying bed, fhe did in a moft lively ard affecting manner exprefs her hope
and joy in the views of approaching glory.
Yet amidft all the triumph of fuch a profpect, there was one remaining care and diftrefs which lay heavy on her mind ; which
was, that as her journey and her ftock of
provifions were both ended together, fhe
feared that fhe muft either be buried at the
parifh expenfe, or leave her moft dutiful and
affectionate daughters the houfe ftripped of
fome of the few moveables which remained
in it, to perform the laft office of duty to
her, which fhe had reafon to believe they
wou'd do.   While fhe was combating with
this only remaining anxiety, I happened,
                                    though

though I knew not the extremity of her illnefs, to come in, and to bring with me a
guinea, which the generous Colonel had fent
by a fpecial meffage, on hearing the character of the family, for its relief.　A prefent
like this, (probably the moft confiderable
they had ever received in their lives) coming in this manner from an entire ftranger,
at fuch a crifis of time, threw my dying friend
(for fuch, amidft all her poverty, I rejoiced
to call her) into a perfect tranfport of joy.
She efteemed it a fingular favour of providence, fent to her in her laft moments, as *a
token of good*, and greeted it as a fpecial mark
of that *loving kindnefs of God*, which fhould
attend her forever.　She would therefore be
raifed up in her bed, that fhe might blefs
God for it upon her knees, and with her laft
breath pray for her kind and generous benefactor, and for him who had been the inftrument of directing his bounty into this
channel.　After which fhe foon expired,
with fuch tranquillity and fweetnefs, as could
not but moft fenfibly delight all who beheld her, and occafioned many, who knew
the circumftances, to *glorify God on her be-
half*.

The Colonel's laft refidence at Northampton was in June and July, 1742, when Lord
Cadogan's regiment of dragoons was quartered

tered here : And I cannot but obferve, that wherever that regiment came, it was remarkable, not only for the fine appearance it made, and for the exactnefs with which it performed its various exercifes, (of which it had about this time the honour to receive the moft illuftrious teftimonials) but alfo for the great fobriety and regularity of the foldiers. Many of the officers copied after the excellent pattern, which they had daily before their eyes, and a confiderable number of the private men feemed to be perfons, not only of ftrict virtue, but of ferious piety. And I doubt not, but they found their abundant account in it ; not only in the ferenity and happinefs of their own minds, which is beyond comparifon the moft important confideration ; but alfo, in fome degree, in the obliging and refpectful treatment which they generally met with in their quarters. And I mention this, becaufe I am perfuaded, that if gentlemen of their profeffion knew, and would reflect, how much more comfortable they make their own quarters, by a fober, orderly, and obliging conduct, they would be regular out of mere felf love ; if they were not influenced, as I heartily wifh they may always be, by a nobler principle.

Towards

Towards the latter end of this year he embarked for Flanders, and spent some confiderable time with the regiment at Ghent ; where he much regretted the want of thofe religious ordinances and opportunities which had made his other abodes delightful.   But as he had made fo eminent a progrefs in that divine life, which they are all intended to promote, he could not be unactive in the caufe of God.   I have now before me a letter dated from thence, October, 16, 1742, in which he writes, " As for me, I am indeed " in a dry and barren land, where no water is. " Rivers of waters run down mine eyes, be- " caufe nothing is to be heard in our Sod- " om, but blafpheming the name of my " God ; and I am not honoured as the in- " ftrument of doing any great fervice.   It is " true, I have reformed fix or feven field " officers of fwearing, I dine every day with " them, and have entered them into a vol- " untary contract, to pay a fhilling to the " poor for every oath ; and it is wonderful " to obferve the effect it has had already. " One of them told me this day at dinner, " that it had really fuch an influence upon " him, that being at cards laft night when " another officer fell a fwearing, he was not " able to bear it, but rofe up and left the " company.   So you fee, reftraints at firft
                              " arifing

" arifing from a low principle, may improve
" into fomething better."

, During his abode here, he had a great
deal of bufinefs upon his hands; and had
alfo, in fome marches, the care of more regiments than his own : And it has been very
delightful to me to obferve, what a degree
of converfe with heaven, and the God of it,
he maintained, amidft thefe fcenes of hurry
and fatigue ; of which the reader may find
a remarkable fpecimen in the following letter, dated from Lichwick, in the beginning
of April, 1743, which was one of the laft I
received from him while abroad, and begins
with thefe words : " Yefterday being the
" Lord's day, at fix in the morning, I had
" the pleafure of receiving yours at Norto-
" nick; and it proved a Sabbath day's bleff-
" ing to me. Some time before it reached
" me," (from whence by the way it may be
obferved, that his former cuftom of rifing fo
early to his devotions was ftill retained) " I
" had been *wreftling with God* with many
" tears ; and when I had read it, I returned
" to my knees again, to give hearty thanks
" to him for all his goodnefs to you and
" yours, and alfo to myfelf, in that he hath
" been pleafed to ftir up fo many who are
" dear to him, to be mindful of me at the
" throne of grace." And then, after the

O　　　　　mention

mention of fome other particulars, he adds,
" Bleffed and adored forever, be the holy
" name of my heavenly father, who holds
" my foul in life, and my body in perfect
" health ! Were I to recount his mercy and
" goodnefs to me, even in the midft of all
" thefe hurries, I fhould never have done.—
" I hope your mafter will ftill encourage
" you in his work, and make you a bleffing
" to many. My deareft friend, I am much
" more yours than I can exprefs, and fhall
" remain fo while I am   J. G."
    In this correfpondence I had a farther
opportunity of difcovering that humble *re-*
fignation to the will of God, which made fo
amiable a part of his character, and of which
before I had feen fo many inftances. He
fpeaks, in the letter from which I have juft
been giving an extract, of the hope he had
expreffed in a former, of feeing us again that
winter; and he adds, " To be fure it would
" have been a great pleafure to me : But we
" poor mortals form projects, and the al-
" mighty ruler of the univerfe difpofes of all
" as he pleafes. A great many of us were
" getting ready for our return to England,
" when we received an order to march to-
" wards Frankfort, to the great furprife of the
" whole army ; neither can any of us com-
" prehend what we are to do there, for there
                                    " is

" is no enemy in that country, the French
" army being marched into Bavaria, where
" I am sure we cannot follow them.   But it
" is *the will of the Lord*, and *his will be done !*
" I desire to bless and praise my heavenly
" father that I am entirely resigned to it.
" It is no matter where I go, or what be-
" comes of me, so that *God may be glorified*
" in my life or my death.   I should rejoice
" much to hear, that all my friends were e-
" qually resigned."

The mention of this article reminds me
of another, relating to the views which he
had of obtaining a regiment for himself.
He endeavoured to deserve it by the most
faithful services ; some of them indeed beyond what the strength of his constitution
would well bear :. For the weather in some
of these marches proved exceeding bad, and
yet he would be always at the head of his
people, that he might look to every thing
that concerned them, with the exactest care.
This obliged him to neglect the beginnings
of a feverish illness ; the natural consequence
of which was, that it grew very formidable,
forced a long confinement upon him, and
gave animal nature a shock which it never
recovered.

In the mean time, as he had the promise
of a regiment before he quitted England, his
friends

friends were continually expecting an occasion of congratulating him on having received the command of one. But still they were disappointed; and on some of them the disappointment seemed to sit heavy. As for the Colonel himself, he seemed quite easy about it; and appeared much greater in that easy situation of mind, than the highest military honours and preferments could have made him. With great pleasure do I at this moment recollect the unaffected serenity, and even indifference, with which he expresses himself upon this occasion, in a letter to me, dated about the beginning of April, 1743. "The disappointment of a "regiment is nothing to me; for I am sat- "isfied that had it been for God's glory, I "should have had it; and I should have "been sorry to have had it on any other "terms. My heavenly father has bestowed "upon me infinitely more than if he had "made me Emperor of the whole world."

I find several parallel expressions in other letters; and those to his lady about the same time, were just in the same strain. In an extract from one which was written from Aix la Chapelle, April 21, the same year, I meet with these words: "People here im- "agine I must be sadly troubled, that I "have not got a regiment, for six out of

"seven

" feven vacant are now difpofed of ; but
" they are ftrangely miftaken, for it has giv-
" en me no fort of trouble : My heavenly
" father knows what is beft for me ; and
" bleffed and forever adored be his name,
" he has given me an entire refignation to
" his will : Befides, I do not know that ever
" I met with any difappointment fince I
" was a Chriftian, but it pleafed God to dif-
" cover to me, that it was plainly for my ad-
" vantage, by beftowing fomething better
" upon me afterwards : Many inftances of
" which I am able to produce ; and there-
" fore I fhould be the greateft of monfters,
" if I did not truft in him."

I fhould be guilty of a great omiffion, if I
were not to add, how remarkably the event
correfponded with his faith, on this occafion.
For whereas he had no intimation, or expectation, of any thing more than a regiment
of foot, his Majefty was pleafed, out of his
great goodnefs, to give him a regiment of
dragoons, which was then quartered juft in
his own neighbourhood. And it is properly
remarked by the reverend and worthy perfon through whofe hands this letter was
tranfmitted to me, that when the Colonel
thus expreffed himfelf, he could have no
profpect of what he afterwards fo foon obtained ; as General Bland's regiment, to

which

which he was advanced, was only vacant on the 19th of April, that is, two days before the date of this letter, when it was impoffible he fhould have any notice of that vacancy. And it alfo deferves obfervation, that fome few days after the Colonel was thus unexpectedly promoted to the command of thefe dragoons, Brigadier Cornwallis's regiment of foot, then in Flanders, became vacant : Now had this happened before his promotion to General Bland's, Colonel Gardiner, in all probability would only have had that regiment of foot, and fo have continued in Flanders. When the affair was iffued, he informs Lady Frances of it, in a letter dated from a village near Frankfort, May 3, in which he refers to his former of the 21ft of April, obferving how remarkably it was verified "in God's having given him," (for fo he expreffes it, agreeably to the views he continually maintained of the univerfal agency of divine providence) " what he had " no expectation of, and what was fo much " better than that which he had miffed, a " regiment of dragoons quartered at his own " door."

It appeared to him that by this remarkable event providence called him home. Accordingly, though he had other preferments offered him, in the army, he chofe to return, and

and I believe the more willingly, as he did not expect there would have been an action. Juſt at this time it pleaſed God to give him an awful inſtance of the uncertainty of human proſpects and enjoyments, by that violent fever, which ſeized him at Ghent in his way to England, and perhaps the more ſeverely, for the efforts he made to puſh on his journey, though he had for ſome days been much indiſpoſed. It was, I think, one of the firſt fits of ſevere illneſs he had ever met with ; and he was ready to look upon it, as a ſudden call into eternity : But it gave him no painful alarm in that view. He committed himſelf to the God of his life, and in a few weeks he was ſo well recovered, as to be capable of purſuing his journey, though not without difficulty : And I cannot but think, it might have conduced much to a more perfect recovery than he ever attained, to have allowed himſelf a longer repoſe, in order to recruit his exhauſted ſtrength and ſpirits. But there was an activity in his temper, not eaſy to be reſtrained ; and it was now ſtimulated, not only by a deſire of ſeeing his friends, but of being with his regiment ; that he might omit nothing in his power, to regulate their morals and their diſcipline, and to form them for public ſervice. Accordingly he paſſed

through

through London about the middle of June, 1743, where he had the honour of waiting on their Royal Highneſſes the Prince and Princeſs of Wales, and of receiving from both the moſt obliging tokens of favour and eſteem.   He arrived at Northampton on Monday the 20th of June, and ſpent part of three days here.   But the great pleaſure which his return and preferment gave us, was much abated, by obſerving his countenance ſo ſadly altered, and the many marks of languor, and remaining diſorder, which evidently appeared ; ſo that he really looked ten years older, than he had done ten months before.   I had however a ſatisfaction, ſufficient to counterbalance much of the concern which this alteration gave me, in a renewed opportunity of obſerving, indeed more ſenſibly than ever, in how remarkable a degree he was dead to the enjoyments and views of this mortal life.   When I congratulated him on the favourable appearances of providence for him in the late event, he briefly told me the remarkable circumſtances that attended it, with the moſt genuine impreſſions of gratitude to God for them ; but added, " that as his account was increaſed " with his income, power, and influence, and " his cares were proportionably increaſed, " it was as to his own perſonal concern much

" the

" the fame to him, whether he had remained
" in his former ftation, or been elevated to
" this ; but that if God fhould by this means
" honour him, as an inftrument of doing
" more good than he could otherwife have
" done, he fhould rejoice in it."

I perceived that the near views he had
taken of eternity, in the illnefs from which
he was then fo imperfectly recovered, had
not in the leaft alarmed him ; but that he
would have been entirely willing, had fuch
been the determination of God, to have
been cut fhort in a foreign land, without
any earthly friend near him, and in the
midft of a journey, undertaken with hopes
and profpects fo pleafing to nature ; which
appeared to me no inconfiderable evidence
of the ftrength of his faith.   But we fhall
wonder the lefs at this extraordinary refignation, if we confider the joyful and aſſured
profpect which he had of an happinefs infinitely fuperior beyond the grave ; of which
that worthy minifter of the church of Scotland, who had an opportunity of converfing
with him quickly after his return, and having the memorable ftory of his converfion
from his own mouth, as I have hinted above,
writes thus in his letter to me, dated Jan.
14, 1746-7.   " When he came to review his
" regiment at Linlithgow in fummer 1743,
                                " after

" after having given me the wonderful flory
" as above, he concluded in words to this
" purpofe : Let me die, whenever it fhall
" pleafe God, or wherever it fhall be, I am
" fure I fhall go to the manfions of eternal
" glory, and enjoy my God and my redeem-
" er in heaven forever."

While he was with us at this time, he appeared deeply affected with the fad ftate of
things as to religion and morals ; and feemed to apprehend, that the rod of God was
hanging over fo finful a nation. He obferved a great deal of difaffection, which the
enemies of the government had, by a variety
of artifices, been raifing in Scotland for fome
years ; and the number of Jacobites there,
together with the defencelefs ftate in which
our ifland then was, with refpect to the
number of its forces at home, (of which he
fpoke at once with great concern and aftonifhment) led him to expect an invafion from
France, and an attempt in favour of the pretender, much fooner than it happened. I
have heard him fay, many years before it
came fo near being accomplifhed, " that a
" few thoufands might have a fair chance for
" marching from Edinburgh to London un-
" controlled, and throw the whole kingdom
" into an aftonifhment." And I have great
reafon to believe, that this was one main
                          confideration,

confideration, which engaged him to make
fuch hafte to his regiment, then quartered in
thofe parts ; as he imagined there was not a
fpot of ground, where he might be more like
to have a call to expofe his life in the fervice of his country ; and perhaps, by appearing on a proper call early in its defence,
be inftrumental in fuppreffing the beginnings of moft formidable mifchief.   How
rightly he judged in thefe things, the event
did too evidently fhew.

The evening before our laft feparation, as
I knew I could not entertain the invaluable
friend who was then my gueft more agreeably, I preached a fermon in my own houfe,
with fome peculiar reference to his cafe and
circumftances, from thofe ever memorable
words, than which I have never felt any
more powerful and more comfortable : Pfal.
xci. 14, 15, 16. *Becaufe he hath fet his love
upon me, therefore will I deliver him ; I will
fet him on high, becaufe he hath known my
name : He fhall call upon me, and I will anfwer him : I will be with him in trouble, I
will deliver him, and honour him : With long
life (or length of days) will I fatisfy him, and
fhew him my falvation.* This fcripture could
not but lead our meditations to furvey the
character of the good man, as one who fo
knows the name of the bleffed God, (has fuch
a deep

a deep apprehenfion of the glories and perfections of his nature) as determinately *to fet
his love upon him*, to make him the fupreme
object of his moft ardent and conftant affection.   And it fuggefted the moft fublime
and animating hopes to perfons of fuch a
character ; that their prayers fhall be always
acceptable unto God ; that though they
may, and muft, be called out to their fhare
in the troubles and calamities of life, yet they
may affure themfelves of the divine prefence
in all ; which fhall iffue in their deliverance,
in their exaltation, fometimes to diftinguifhed honour and efteem among men, and, it
may be, in a long courfe of ufeful and happy years on earth at leaft, which fhall undoubtedly end in feeing, to their perpetual
delight, the complete falvation of God, in a
world where they fhall enjoy *length of days
forever and ever*, and employ them all in
adoring the great author of their falvation
and felicity.   It is evident, that thefe natural thoughts on fuch a fcripture, were matters of univerfal concern.   Yet had I known
that this was the laft time I fhould ever addrefs Colonel Gardiner, as a minifter of the
gofpel, and had I forefeen the fcenes through
which God was about to lead him, I hardly
know what confiderations I could have fuggefted with more peculiar propriety.   The
attention,

attention, elevation, and delight, with which he heard them, was very apparent; and the pleafure which the obfervation of it gave me, continues to this moment. And let me be permitted to digrefs fo far, as to add, that this is indeed the great fupport of a Chriftian minifter, under the many difcouragements and difappointments which he meets with, in his attempts to fix upon the profligate or the thoughtlefs part of mankind a deep fenfe of religious truth; that there is another important part of his work, in which he may hope to be more generally fuccefsful; as by plain, artlefs, but ferious difcourfes, the great principles of Chriftian duty and hope may be nourifhed and invigorated in good men, their graces watered as at the root, and their fouls animated both to perfevere and improve in hólinefs: And when we are effectually performing fuch benevolent offices, fo well fuiting our immortal natures, to perfons whofe hearts are cemented with ours in the bonds of the moft endearing and facred friendfhip, it is too little to fay it overpays the fatigue of our labours; it even fwallows up all fenfe of it, in the moft rational and fublime pleafure.

An incident occurs to my mind, which happened that evening, which at leaft for

the oddnefs of it may deferve a place in
thefe memoirs.   I had then with me one
Thomas Porter, a poor, but very honeft and
religious man, now living at Hatfield Broad-
oak in Effex, who is quite unacquainted
with letters, fo as not to be able to diftinguifh one from another; yet is mafter of
the contents of the Bible in fo extraordinary
a degree, that he has not only fixed an im-
menfe number of texts in his memory, but
merely by hearing them quoted in fermons
has regiftered there the chapter and verfe, in
which thefe paffages are to be found : This
is attended with a marvellous facility in directing thofe that can read, to turn to them,
and a moft unaccountable talent for fixing
on fuch as fuit almoft every imaginable variety of circumftances in common life.
There are two confiderations in his cafe,
which make it the more wonderful : The
one, that he is a perfon of a very low genius, having, befides a ftammering, which
makes his fpeech almoft unintelligible to
ftrangers, fo wild and aukward a manner of
behaviour, that he is frequently taken for an
idiot, and feems in many things to be indeed
fo : The other, that he grew up to manhood
in a very licentious courfe of living, and an
entire ignorance of divine things, fo that all
thefe exact impreffions on his memory have

been

been made in his riper years.   I thought it
would not be difagreeable to the Col. to introduce to him this odd phenomenon, which
many hundreds of people have had a curiofity to examine : And among all the ftrange
things I have feen in him, I never remember any which equalled what paffed on this
occafion.   On hearing the Colonel's profeffion, and receiving fome hints of his religious charaﬆer, he ran through a vaﬆ variety of fcriptures, beginning at the Penta-
teuch and going on to the Revelation, relating either to the dependence to be fixed
on God for the fuccefs of military preparations, or to the inﬆances and promifes occurring there of his care of good men in the
moﬆ imminent dangers, or to the encouragement to defpife perils and death, while
engaged in a good caufe, and fupported by
the views of a happy immortality.   I believe he quoted more than twenty of thefe
paffages ; and I muﬆ freely own, that I
know not who could have chofe them with
greater propriety.   If my memory doth not
deceive me, the laﬆ of this catalogue was
that from which I afterwards preached on
the lamented occafion of this great man's
fall : *Be thou faithful unto death, and I will
give thee a crown of life.*   We were all aftonifhed at fo remarkable a faﬆ ; and I
                                   queﬆion

queftion not, but that many of my readers will think the memory of it worthy of being thus preferved.

But to return to my main fubject : The next day after the fermon and converfation of which I have been fpeaking, I took my laft leave of my ineftimable friend, after attending him fome part of his way northward. 'I he firft ftage of our journey was to the cottage of that poor, but very religious family, which I had occafion to mention above, as relieved, and indeed in a great meafure fubfifted, by his charity. And nothing could be more delightful, than to obferve the condefcenfion, with which he converfed with thefe his humble penfioners. We there put up our laft united prayers together ; and he afterwards expreffed in the ftrongeft terms I ever heard him ufe on fuch an occafion, the fingular pleafure with which he had joined in them. Indeed it was no fmall fatisfaction to me, to have an opportunity of recommending fuch a valuable friend to the divine protection and bleffing, with that particular freedom, and enlargement on what was peculiar in his circumftances, which hardly any other fituation, unlefs we had been quite alone, could fo conveniently have admitted. We went from thence to the table of a perfon of dif-
.tinction

tinction in the neighbourhood; where he
had an opportunity of shewing, in how decent and graceful a manner he could unite
the Christian and the gentleman, and give
conversation an improving and religious
turn, without violating any of the rules of
polite behaviour, or saying or doing any
thing which looked at all constrained or affected.   Here we took our last embrace,
committing each other to the care of the God
of heaven ; and the Colonel pursued his
journey to the north, where he spent all the
remainder of his days.

The more I reflect upon this appointment of providence, the more I discern of
the beauty and wisdom of it ; not only as it
led directly to that glorious period of life,
with which God had determined to honour
him, and in which I think, it becomes all
his friends to rejoice ; but also, as the retirement on which he entered, could not but
have a happy tendency to favour his more
immediate and complete preparation for so
speedy a remove.   To which we may add,
that it must probably have a very powerful
influence to promote the interests of religion (incomparably the greatest of all interests) among the members of his own family ;
who must surely edify much by such daily
lessons as they received from his lips, when

they

they faw them illuftrated and enforced by
fo admirable an example, and this for two
complete years. It is the more remarkable,
as I cannot find from the memoirs of his life
in my hands, that he had ever been fo long
at home fince he had a family, or indeed,
from his childhood, ever fo long at a time
in any one place.

With how clear a luftre his lamp fhone,
and with what holy vigour his loins were
girded up in the fervice of his God, in thefe
his latter days, I learn in part from the letters of feveral excellent perfons, in the miniftry, or in fecular life, with whom I have
fince converfed or correfponded. And in
his many letters dated from Bankton during
this period, I have ftill farther evidence how
happy he was, amidft thofe infirmities of
body, which his tendernefs for me would
feldom allow him to mention; for it appears from them, what a daily intercourfe
he kept up with heaven, and what delightful communion with God crowned his attendance on publick ordinances, and his
fweet hours of devout retirement. He
mentions his facramental opportunities with
peculiar relifh, crying out as in a holy rapture, in reference to one and another of
them, " O how gracious a mafter do we
" ferve ! how pleafant is his fervice ! how
" rich

" rich the entertainments of his love! yet,
" oh how poor and cold are our fervices!"
But I will not multiply quotations of this
fort, after thofe I have given above, which
may be a fufficient fpecimen of many more
in the fame ftrain. This hint may fuffice
to fhew, that the fame ardour of foul held
out in a great meafure to the laft; and
indeed it feems, that towards the clofe of
life, like the flame of a lamp almoft expiring, it fometimes exerted an unufual blaze.

He fpent much of his time at Bankton in
religious folitude; and one moft intimately
converfant with him affures me, that the
traces of that delightful converfe with God,
which he enjoyed in it, might eafily be difcerned in that folemn yet cheerful countenance, with which he often came out of his
clofet. Yet his exercifes there muft fometimes have been very mournful, confidering
the melancholy views which he had of the
ftate of our publick affairs. " I fhould be
" glad," fays he, in a letter which he fent
me about the clofe of the year 1743, " to
" hear what wife and good people among
" you think of the prefent circumftances of
" things. For my own part, though I thank
" God I fear nothing for myfelf, my appre-
" henfions for the publick are very gloomy,
" confidering the deplorable prevalency of
" almoft

" almoſt all kinds of wickedneſs amongſt us ;
" the natural conſequence of the contempt
" of the goſpel. I am daily offering my
" prayers to God for this ſinful land of ours,
" over which his judgments ſeem to be gath-
" ering ; and my ſtrength is ſometimes ſo ex-
" hauſted with thoſe ſtrong cries and tears
" which I pour out before God on this oc-
" caſion, that I am hardly able to ſtand when
" I ariſe from my knees." If we have
many remaining to ſtand in the breach with
equal fervency, I hope, crying as our prov-
ocations are, God will ſtill be intreated for
us, and ſave us.

Moſt of the other letters I had the pleaſure of receiving from him after our laſt ſep-
aration, are either filled, like thoſe of former
years, with tender expreſſions of affectionate
ſolicitude for my domeſtic comfort and publick uſefulneſs, or relate to the writings I
publiſhed during this time, or to the affairs
of his eldeſt ſon then under my care. But
theſe are things, which are by no means of
a nature to be communicated here. It is
enough to remark in the general, that the
Chriſtian was ſtill mingled with all the care
of the friend and the parent.

But I think it incumbent upon me to obſerve, that during this time, and ſome preceding years, his attention, ever wakeful to

ſuch

such concerns, was much engaged by some religious appearances, which happened about this time, both in England and Scotland ; with regard to which some may be curious to know his sentiments. He communicated them to me with the most unreserved freedom ; and I cannot apprehend myself under any engagements to conceal them, as I am persuaded that it will be no prejudice to his memory that they should be publickly known.

It was from Colonel Gardiner's pen that I received the first notice of that ever memorable scene which was opened at Kylsyth, under the ministry of the Rev. Mr. MacCulloch, in the month of February, 1741-2. He communicated to me the copy of two letters from that eminently favoured servant of God, giving an account of that extraordinary success which had within a few days accompanied his preaching ; when, as I remember, in a little more than a fortnight, a hundred and thirty souls, who had before continued in long insensibility under the faithful preaching of the gospel, were awakened on a sudden to attend it, as if it had been a new revelation brought down from heaven, and attested by as astonishing miracles as ever were wrought by Peter or Paul ; though they heard it only from a person,
                                        under

under whofe miniftry they have fate for feveral years. Struck with a power and majefty in the word of God, which they had never felt before, they crowded his houfe night and day, making their applications to him for fpiritual direction and affiftance, with an earneftnefs and folicitude, which floods of tears and cries, that fwallowed up their own words and his, could not fufficiently exprefs. The Colonel mentioned this at firft to me, " as matter of eternal praife, which he knew would rejoice my very foul :" And when he faw it fpread in the neighbouring parts, and obferved the glorious reformation which it produced in the lives of great multitudes, and the abiding fruits of it for fucceeding months and years, it increafed and confirmed his joy. But the facts relating to this matter have been laid before the world in fo authentic a manner, and the *agency of divine grace* in them has been fo rationally vindicated, and fo pathetically reprefented, in what the reverend and judicious Mr. Webfter has written upon that fubject ; that it is altogether fuperfluous for me to add any thing farther than my hearty prayers, that the work may be as extenfive as it was apparently glorious and divine.

It

It was with great pleafure that he received any intelligence of a like kind from England ; whether the clergy of the eftablifhed
church or diffenting minifters, whether our
own countrymen or foreigners, were the inftruments of it.   And whatever weakneffes
or errors might mingle themfelves with valuable qualities in fuch as were active in fuch
a work, he appeared to love and honour
them, in proportion to the degree he faw
reafon to believe their hearts were devoted
to the fervice of Chrift, and their attempts
owned and fucceeded by him.   I remember
that mentioning one of thefe gentlemen,
who had been remarkably fuccefsful in his
miniftry, and feemed to have met with
fome unkind ufage, he fays, " I had rather
" be *that defpifed perfecuted man*, to be an
" inftrument in the hand of the fpirit, in
" converting fo many fouls, and building up
" fo many in their holy faith, than I would
" be Emperor of the whole world."   Yet
this fteady and judicious Chriftian, (for fuch
he moft affuredly was) at the fame time that
he efteemed a man for his good intention
and his worthy qualities, did not fuffer himfelf to be hurried away into all the fingular-
ity of his fentiments, or to admire his im-
prudences or exceffes.   On the contrary, he
faw and lamented that artifice which the
great

great father of fraud has fo long and fo fuc_
cefsfully been practifing; who, like the en_
emies of Ifrael, when he cannot entirely
prevent the building of God's temple, does
as it were offer his affiftance to carry on the
work, that he may thereby get the moft ef_
fectual opportunities of obftructing it. The
Colonel often expreffed his aftonifhment at
the wide extremes into which fome, whom
on the whole he thought very good men,
were permitted to run in many doctrinal
and fpeculative points; and difcerned how
evidently it appeared from hence, that we
cannot argue the truth of any doctrine from
the fuccefs of the preacher; fince this would
be a kind of demonftration, (if I may be al_
lowed the expreffion) which might equally
prove both parts of a contradiction. Yet
when he obferved, that an high regard to the
atonement and righteoufnefs of Chrift, and
to the free grace of God in him, exerted by
the operation of the divine fpirit, was gen_
erally common to all who had been peculi_
arly fuccefsful in the converfion and refor_
mation of men, (how widely foever their
judgments might differ in other points, and
how warmly foever they might oppofe each
other in confequence of that diverfity;) it
tended greatly to confirm his faith in thefe
principles, as well as to open his heart in
                                        love

love to all of every denomination, who maintained an affectionate regard to them. And though what he remarked as to the conduct and fuccefs of minifters of the moft oppofite ftrains of preaching, confirmed him in thefe fentiments ; yet he always efteemed and loved virtuous and benevolent men, even where he thought them moft miftaken in the notions they formed of religion, or in the methods by which they attempted to ferve it.

While I thus reprefent what all who knew him muft foon have obferved of Colonel Gardiner's affectionate regard to thefe peculiar doctrines of our holy religion, it is neceffary that I fhould alfo inform my reader, that it was not his judgment, that the attention of minifters or their hearers fhould be wholly ingroffed by thefe, excellent as they are ; but that all the parts of the fcheme of truth and duty fhould be regarded in their due connection and proportion.   Far from that diftempered tafte, which can bear nothing but cordials, it was his deliberate judgment that the law fhould be preached as well as the gofpel ; and hardly any thing gave him greater offence, than the irreverent manner in which fome, who have been ignorantly extolled as the moft zealous evangelical preachers, have fometimes been

Q   tempted

tempted to speak of the former; much indeed to the scandal of all confistent and judicious Christians. He delighted to be instructed in his duty, and to hear much of the inward exercises of the spiritual and divine life. And he always wished, so far as I could observe, to have these topics treated in a rational as well as a spiritual manner, with solidity and order of thought, with perspicuity and weight of expression; as well knowing, that religion is a most reasonable service; that God has not chosen idiots or lunatics as the inftruments, or nonsense as the means of building up his church; and that though the charge of enthufiafm is often fixed on christianity and its ministers, in a wild, undeferved, and indeed (on the whole) enthufiaftical manner, by some of the loudest or most folemn pretenders to reafon; yet there is really such a thing as enthufiafm, againft which it becomes the true friends of the revelation to be diligently on their guard, left christianity inftead of being exalted, should be greatly corrupted and debafed, and all manner of abfurdity, both in doctrine and practice, introduced by methods, which, like perfecution, throw truth and falfehood on a level, and render the groffeft errors at once more plaufible and incurable. He had too much candour and equity to fix

general

general charges of this nature ; but he was really, and I think not vainly, apprehensive that the emissaries and agents of the most corrupt church that ever dishonoured the Christian name, (by which it will easily be understood, I mean that of Rome) might very possibly insinuate themselves into societies, to which they could not otherwise have access, and make their advantage of that total resignation of the understanding, and contempt of reason and learning, which nothing but ignorance, delirium, or knavery, can dictate, to lead men blindfold whither it pleased, till it set them down at the foot of an altar, where transubstantiation itself is consecrated. I know not where I can more properly introduce another part of the Colonel's character, which, obvious as it was, I have not yet touched upon ; I mean his tenderness to those who were under any spiritual distress ; wherein he was indeed an example to ministers, in a duty more peculiarly theirs. I have seen many amiable instances of this myself ; and I have been informed of many others : One of which happened about the time of that awakening in the western parts of Scotland; which I touched upon above ; when the Rev. Mr. Mac Laurin, of Glasgow, found occasion to witness to the great propriety,

judgment,

judgment, and felicity of manner, with which he addreſſed ſpiritual conſolation to an afflicted ſoul, who applied to the profeſſ- or, at a time when he had not an opportu- nity immediately to give audience to the caſe. And indeed as long ago as the year 1726, I find him writing to a friend in a ſtrain of tenderneſs in this regard, which might well have become the moſt affection- ate and experienced paſtor. He there con- gratulates him on ſome religious enjoyments lately received, (in part it ſeems by his means) when among others he has this mod- eſt expreſſion : " If I have been made any " way the means of doing you good, give " the whole glory to God ; for he has been " willing to ſhew, that *the power* was entire- " ly *of himſelf,* ſince he has been pleaſed to " make uſe of ſo very weak an inſtrument." In the ſame letter he admoniſhes his friend, that he ſhould not be too much ſurpriſed, if after having been, as he expreſſes it, *upon the mount,* he ſhould be brought *into the valley* again ; and reminds him that " we live by " faith, and not by ſenſible aſſurance ;" rep- reſenting, that there are ſome ſuch full com- munications from God as ſeem almoſt to ſwallow up the actings of faith, from whence they take their riſe : " Whereas, when a " Chriſtian who *walks in darkneſs, and ſees*

" *no*

" *no light*, will yet hang (as it were) on the
" report of an abfent Jefus, and," as one expreffes it in allufion to the ftory of Jacob and
Jofeph " can put himfelf, as on *the chariot*
" of the promifes, to be borne on to him,
" whom now he fees not; there may be fub-
" limer and more acceptable actings of a pure
" and ftrong faith, than in moments which
" afford the foul a much more rapturous
" delight." This is the fubftance of what he
fays in the excellent letter. Some of the
phrafes made ufe of, might not perhaps be
intelligible to feveral of my readers, for
which reafon I do not exactly tranfcribe
them all: But this is plainly and fully his
meaning, and moft of the words are his
own. The fentiment is furely very juft and
important; and happy would it be for many
excellent perfons, who through wrong notions of the nature of *faith* (which was never
more mifreprefented than now among fome)
are perplexing themfelves with moft ground-
lefs doubts and fcruples, if it were more
generally underftood, admitted and cofid-
ered.

An endeared friend, who was moft intimately converfant with the Colonel during
the two laft years of his life, has favoured
me with an account of fome little circumftances relating to him; which I efteem as

Q 2   precious

precious fragments, by which the confiftent tenor of his chara&ter may be farther illuf_ trated. I fhall therefore infert them here, without being very folicitous as to the order in which they are introduced.

He perceived himfelf evidently in a very declining ftate from his firft arrival in Brit_ ain, and feemed to entertain a fixed appre_ henfion, that he fhould continue but a little while longer in life. " He expe&ed death," fays my good correfpondent, " and was de_ lighted with the profpe&," which did not grow lefs amiable by a nearer approach. The *word of God*, with which he had as intimate an acquaintance as moft men I ever knew; and on which (efpecially on the New Tef_ tament) I have heard him make many very judicious and accurate remarks, was ftill his daily ftudy; and it furnifhed him with mat_ ter of frequent converfation, much to the edification and comfort of thofe that were about him. It was recolle&ed, that among other paffages he had lately fpoken of the following, as having made a deep impreffion on his mind : *My foul, wait thou only upon God !* He would repeat it again and again, *Only, Only, Only !* So plainly did he fee, and fo deeply did he feel, the vanity of crea_ ture confidences and expe&ations. With the ftrongeft atteftation would he often mention

mention thofe words in Ifaiah, as verified by long experience : *Thou wilt keep him in perfect peace, whofe mind is flayed on thee ; becaufe he trufteth in thee.* And with peculiar fatisfaction would he utter thofe heroic words in Habakkuk, which he found armour of proof againft every fear and every contingency : *Though the fig tree fhall not bloffom, neither fhall fruit be in the vines ; the labour of the olive fhall fail, and the fields fhall yield no meat ; the flocks fhall be cut off from the fold, and there fhall be no herd in the ftalls : Yet I will rejoice in the Lord, I will joy in the God of my falvation.* The cxlvth Pfalm was alfo fpoken of by him with great delight, and Dr. Watts's verfion of it ; as well as feveral other of that excellent perfon's poetical compofures. My friend who tranfmits to me this account, adds the following words, which I defire to infert with the deepeft fentiments of unfeigned humility and felf abafement before God, as moft unworthy the honour of contributing in the leaft degree to the joys and graces of one fo much my fuperior in every part of the Chriftian character. " As the joy with " which good men fee the happy fruits of " their labours, makes a part of the prefent " reward of the fervants of God and the " friends of Jefus, it muft not be omitted,
                              " even

" even in a letter to you, that your fpiritual
" hymns were among his moft delightful
" and foul improving repafts ;. particularly
" thofe, on *beholding tranfgreffors with grief,*
" and Chrift's. *meffage.*" What is added
concerning my book of the *Rife and Prog-*
refs of Religion, and the terms in which he
expreffed his efteem of it, I cannot fuffer to
pafs my pen ; only defire moft fincerely to
blefs God, that efpecially by the laft chapters
of that treatife, I had an opportunity at fo
great a diftance of exhibiting fome offices of
Chriftian friendfhip to this excellent perfon,
in the clofing fcenes of life ; which it would
have been my greateft joy to have performed in perfon, had providence permitted me
then to have been near him.

The former of thofe hymns my correfpondent mentions, as having been fo agreeable to Colonel Gardiner, I have given the
reader above, (fee page 136) the latter, which
is called Chrift's *meffage,*. took its rife from
Luke iv. 18, *& feq,* and is as follows :

I.

HARK ! the glad found ! the Saviour comes,
The Saviour promis'd long !
Let ev'ry heart prepare a throne,
And ev'ry voice a fong.

On

II

On him the fpirit largely pour'd
  Exerts its facred fire :
Wifdom, and might, and zeal, and love,
  His holy breaft infpire.

III

He comes, the prifoners to releafe
  In Satan's bondage held :
The gates of brafs before him burft,
  The iron fetters yield.

IV

He comes, from thickeft films of vice
  To clear the mental ray,
And on the eyeballs of the blind
  To pour celeftial day.*

V

He comes, the broken heart to bind,
  The bleeding foul to cure ;
And with the treafures of his grace
  T' inrich the humble poor.

VI

His filver trumpets publifh loud
  The jub'lee of the Lord ;
Our debts are all remitted now,
  Our heritage reftor'd.

VII

Our glad hofannahs, Prince of Peace,
  Thy welcome fhall proclaim ;
And heav'n's eternal arches ring
  With thy beloved name.

There

* This ftanza is moftly borrowed from Mr. Pope,

There is one hymn more I shall beg leave to add, plain as it is, which Colonel Gardiner has been heard to mention with particular regard, as expressing the inmost sentiments of his soul ; and they were undoubtedly so, in the last rational moments of his expiring life. It is called, *Christ precious to the believer ;* and was composed to be sung after a sermon on 1. Pet. ii. 7.

I

JESUS ! I love thy charming name,.
  'Tis music to my ear :
Fain would I sound it out so loud,
  That earth and heav'n should hear.

II

Yes, thou art precious to my soul,
  My transport and my trust :
Jewels to thee are gaudy toys,
  And gold is sordid dust.

III

All my capacious pow'rs can wish,
  In thee most richly meet :
Nor to my eyes is life so dear,
  Nor friendship half so sweet.

IV

Thy grace still dwells upon my heart,
  And sheds its fragrance there ;
The noblest balm of all its wounds,
  The cordial of its care.

I'll

V

I'll fpeak the honours of thy name
  With my laft lab'ring breath ;
Then fpeechlefs clafp thee in my arms,
  The antidote of death.

· Thofe who were intimate with Colonel
Gardiner, muft have obferved how ready he
was to give a devotional turn to any fubject
that occurred.   And in particular the fpiritual and heavenly difpofition of his foul
difcovered itfelf in the reflections and im-
provements which he made, when reading
hiftory ; in which he took a good deal of
pleafure, as perfons remarkable for their
knowledge of mankind, and obfervation of
providence generally do.   I have an inftance of this before me, which though too
natural to be at all furprifing, will I dare
fay be pleafing to the devout mind.   He
had juft been reading in Rollin's extract
from Xenophon, the anfwer which the lady
of Tigranes made, when all the company
were extolling Cyrus, and expreffing the
admiration with which his appearance and
behaviour ftruck them : The queftion being
afked her, what fhe thought of him ? fhe
anfwered, I don't know, I did not obferve
him.   On what then, faid one of the company, did you fix your attention ? *On him*,
replied fhe, (referring to the generous fpeech
which

which her hufband had juft made) *who faid*
he would give a thoufand lives to ranfom my
liberty. "Oh," cried the Colonel when
reading it, " how ought we to fix our eyes
" and hearts on *him*, who not in offer but in
" reality, *gave his own precious life* to ran-
" fom us from the moft dreadful flavery,
" and from eternal deftruction!" But this is
only one inftance among a thoufand.   His
heart was fo habitually fet upon divine
things, and he had fuch a permanent and
overflowing fenfe of the love of Chrift, that
he could not forbear connecting fuch reflections, with a multitude of more diftant occafions occurring in daily life, where lefs
advanced Chriftians would not have thought
of them : And thus, like our great mafter,
he made every little incident a fource of devotion, and an inftrument of holy zeal.

Enfeebled as his conftitution was, he was
ftill intent on improving his time to fome
valuable purpofes : And when his friends
expoftulated with him, that he gave his body
fo little reft, he ufed to anfwer, " It will reft
" long enough in the grave."

The July before his death, he was perfuaded to take a journey to Scarborough for
the recovery of his health ; from which he
was at leaft encouraged to expect fome little
revival.   After this he had thoughts of going

to

to London, and defigned to have fpent part
of September at Northampton.   The expectation of this was mutually agreeable ;
but providence faw fit to difconcert the
fcheme.   His love for his friends in thefe
parts occafioned him to exprefs fome regret
on his being commanded back : And I am
pretty confident, from the manner in which
he exprefled himfelf in one of his laft letters
to me, that he had fome more important
reafons for wifhing an opportunity of making a London journey juft at that crifis ;
which, the reader will remember, was before
the rebellion broke out.   But as providence
determined it otherwife, he acquiefced ; and
I am well fatisfied, that could he have dif-
tinctly forefeen the approaching event, fo
far as it concerned his own perfon, he would
have efteemed it the happieft fummons he
ever received.   While he was at Scarborough, I find by a letter dated from thence,
July 26, 1745, that he had been informed of
the gaity which fo unfeafonably prevailed at
Edinburgh, where great multitudes were
then fpending their time in balls, affemblies,
and other gay amufements, little mindful of
the rod of God which was then hanging
over them ; on which occafion he hath this
expreffion : " I am greatly furprifed · that
" the people of Edinburgh fhould be em-

R   ployed

" ployed in such foolish diversions, when
" our situation is at present more melan-
" choly than ever I saw it in my life. But
" there is one thing which I am very sure
" of, that comforts me, viz. that it shall *go*
" *well with the righteous*, come what will."

Quickly after his return home, the flame
burst out, and his regiment was ordered to
Stirling.   It was in the castle there that his
lady and eldest daughter enjoyed the last
happy hours of his company ; and I think
it was about eight or ten days before his
death, that he parted from them. A remarkable circumstance attended that part-
ing, which hath been touched upon by sur-
viving friends in more than one of their letters to me.   His lady was so affected when
she took her last leave of him, that she could
not forbear bursting out into a flood of tears,
with other marks of unusual emotion. And
when he asked her the reason, she urged the
apprehension she had of losing such an invaluable friend, amidst the dangers to which
he was then called out, as a very sufficient
apology.   Upon which she took particular
notice, that whereas he had generally comforted her on such occasions, by pleading
with her that remarkable hand of providence, which had so frequently, in former
instances, been exerted for his preservation,

and

and that in the greateſt extremity, he ſaid nothing of it now; but only replied, in his ſententious manner, " We have an eternity " to ſpend together."

That heroic contempt of death, which had often diſcovered itſelf in the midſt of former dangers, was manifeſted now in his diſcourſe with ſeveral of his moſt intimate friends. I have reſerved for this place one genuine ex-preſſion of it many years before, which I tho't might be mentioned with ſome advan-tage here. In July, 1725, he had been ſent to ſome place, not far from Hamilton, to quell a mutiny among ſome of our troops. I know not the particular occaſion; but I remember to have heard him mention it as ſo fierce a one, that he ſ○○○e ever appre-hended himſelf in a more hazardous circum-ſtance. Yet he quelled it by his preſence alone, and the expoſtulations he uſed; e-vidently *putting his life into his hand* to do it. The particulars of the ſtory ſtruck me much; but I do not ſo exactly remember them, as to venture to relate them here. I only obſerve, that in a letter dated July 16, that year, which I have now before me, and which evidently refers to this event, he writes thus: " I have been very buſy, hur-" ried about from place to place; but bleſſ-" ed be God, all is over without bloodſhed.
" And

" And pray let me afk, what made you fhew
" fo much concern for me in your laft ?
" Were you afraid I fhould get to heaven
" before you ? Or can any evil befall thofe
" who are followers of that which is good ?"*

And as thefe were his fentiments in the
vigour of his days, fo neither did declining
years, and the infirmities of a broken conftitution on the one hand, nor any defires
of enjoying the honours and profits of fo
high a ftation, or what was much more to
him, the converfe of the moft affectionate of
wives, and fo many amiable children and
friends on the other, enervate his fpirits in
the leaft : But as he had in former years often expreffed it, to me and feveral others as
his defire, " that if it were the will of God,
" he might have fome honourable call to
                                    " facrifice

* I doubt not but this will remind fome of my readers
of that noble fpeech of Zuinglius, when, according to the
ufage of that country, attending his flock to a battle, in
which their religion and liberties were all at ftake, on his
receiving a mortal wound by a bullet, of which he foon
expired, while his friends were in all the firft aftonifhment
of grief, he bravely faid as he was dying, " Ecquid hoc in-
fortunii ? Is this to be reckoned a misfortune ?" How
many of our deifts would have celebrated fuch a fen-
tence if it had come from the lips of an ancient Roman ?
Strange, that the name of Chrift fhould be fo odious, that
the brighteft virtues of his followers fhould be defpifed for
his fake ! But fo it is ; and fo our mafter told us it would
be : And our faith is in this connection confirmed by
thofe that ftrive moft to overthrow it.

" sacrifice his life in defence of religion and
" the liberties of his country ;" so that when
it appeared to him most probable that he
might be called to it immediately, he met the
summons with the greatest readiness. This
appears in part from a letter which he wrote
to the Rev. Mr. Adams, of Falkirk, just as
he was on marching from Stirling; which
was only eight days before his death : " The
" rebels," says he, " are advancing to cross
" the Firth ; but I trust in the Almighty
" God, *who doth whatsoever he pleases, in the*
" *armies of heaven, and among the inhabitants*
" *of the earth."* And the same gentleman
tells me, that a few days after the date of
this, he marched through Falkirk with his
regiment ; and though he was then in so
languishing a state, that he needed his assist-
ance as a secretary, to write for some reinforcement, which might put it in his power
to make a stand, as he was very desirous to
have done, he expressed a most genuine and
noble contempt of life, when to be exposed
in the defence of a worthy cause.

Thefe sentiments wrought in him to the
last, in the most effectual manner ; and he
seemed for a while to have infused them into
the regiment which he commanded : For
they expressed such a spirit in their march
from Stirling, that I am assured the Colonel

R 2   was

was obliged to exert all his authority to prevent their making incurfions on the rebel
army, which then lay very near them ; and
had it been thought proper to fend him the
reinforcement he requefted, none can fay
what the confequence might have been.
But he was ordered to march as faft as poffible, to meet Sir John Cope's forces at
Dunbar ; which he did : And that hafty
retreat, in concurrence with the news which
they foon after received of the furrender of
Edinburgh to the rebels, (either by the
treachery or weaknefs of a few, in oppofition
to the judgment of by far the greater and
better part of the inhabitants) ftruck a panic
into both the regiments of dragoons, which
became vifible in fome very apparent and
remarkable circumftances in their behaviour, which I forbear to relate.   This affected Colonel Gardiner fo much, that on
the Thurfday before the fatal action at Prefton Pans, he intimated to an officer of confiderable rank and note, (from whom I had
it by a very fure channel of conveyance) that
he expected the event would be, as in fact
it was.   In this view there is all imaginable
reafon to believe he had formed his refolution as to his own perfonal conduct, which
was, " that he would not, in cafe of the
" flight of thofe under his command, retreat
                                      " with

"with them ;" by which, as it feemed, he was reafonably apprehenfive he might have ftained the honour of his former fervices, and have given fome occafion for the enemy to have fpoken reproachfully. He much rather chofe, if providence gave him the call, to leave in his death an example of fidelity and bravery, which might very probably be (as in fact it feems indeed to have been) of much greater importance to his country, than any other fervice, which in the few days of remaining life he could expect to render it. I conclude thefe to have been his views, not only from what I knew of his general character and temper, but likewife from fome intimations which he gave to a very worthy perfon from Edinburgh, who vifited him the day before the action ; to whom he faid, " I cannot influ-" ence the conduct of others, as I could wifh, " but I have one life to facrifice to my coun-" try's fafety, and I fhall not fpare it ;" or words to that effect.

I have heard fuch a multitude of inconfiftent reports of the circumftances of Colonel Gardiner's death, that I had almoft defpaired of being able to give my reader any particular fatisfaction concerning fo interefting a fcene. But by a happy accident I have very lately had an opportunity of being

ing exactly informed of the whole, by that brave man Mr. John Foster, his faithful servant, (and worthy of the honour of serving such a master,) whom I had seen with him at my house some years before. He attended him in his last hours, and gave me the narration at large ; which he would be ready, if it were requisite, to attest upon oath. From his mouth I wrote it down with the utmost exactness, and could easily believe from the genuine and affectionate manner in which he related the particulars, that according to his own striking expression, "his eye and his heart were always "upon his honoured master during the whole time."*

On Friday, September 20, (the day before the battle which transmitted him to his immortal crown,) when the whole army was drawn up, I think about noon, the Colonel rode through all the ranks of his own regiment, addressing them at once in the most respectful and animating manner, both

as

* Just as I am putting the last hand to these memoirs, March 2, 1746-7, I have met with a corporal in Colonel Lascelles's regiment, who was also an eye witness to what happened at Preston Pans on the day of the battle, and the day before : And the account he has given me of some memorable particulars, is so exactly agreeable to that which I received from Mr. Foster, that it would much corroborate his testimony, if there were not so many other considerations to render it convincing.

as soldiers, and as Christians, to engage them to exert themselves courageously in the service of their country, and to neglect nothing that might have a tendency to prepare them for whatever event might happen. They seemed much affected with the address, and expressed a very ardent desire of attacking the enemy immediately : A desire in which he and another very gallent officer of distinguished rank, dignity, and character, both for bravery and conduct, would gladly have gratified them if it had been in the power of either. He earnestly pressed it on the commanding officer, both as the soldiers were then in better spirits than it could be supposed they would be after having passed the night under arms ; and also as the circumstance of making an attack would be some encouragement to them, and probably some terror to the enemy, who would have had the disadvantage of standing on their defence : A disadvantage, with which those wild barbarians (for such most of them were) perhaps would have been more struck than better disciplined troops ; especially, when they fought against the laws of their country too. He also apprehended, that by marching to meet them, some advantage might have been secured with regard to the ground ;

with

with which, it is natural to imagine, he muſt have been perfectly acquainted, as it lay juſt at his own door, and he had rode over it ſo many hundred times. When I mention theſe things, I do not pretend to be capable of judging how far this advice was on the whole right. A variety of cir-cumſtances, to me unknown, might make it otherwiſe. It is certain however, that it was brave. But it was overruled in this reſpect, as it alſo was in the diſpoſition of the cannon, which he would have had plant-ed in the centre of our ſmall army, rather than juſt before his regiment, which was in the right wing ; where he was apprehenſive the horſes, which had not been in any en-gagement before, might be thrown into ſome diſorder by the diſcharge ſo very near them. He urged this the more, as he thought the attack of the rebels might probably be made on the centre of the foot ; where he knew there were ſome brave men, on whoſe ſtand-ing he thought under God the ſucceſs of the day depended. When he found that he could not carry either of theſe points, nor ſome others, which out of regard to the common ſafety he inſiſted upon with ſome unuſual earneſtneſs, he dropped ſome inti-mations of the conſequences which he ap-prehended, and which did in fact follow ;

and

and fubmitting to providence, fpent the remainder of the day in making as good a difpofition, as circumftances would allow.*

He continued all night under arms, wrapped up in his cloak, and generally fheltered
under a rick of barley which happened to
be in the field. About three in the morning, he called his domeftic fervants to him,
of which there were four in waiting. He
difmiffed three of them, with moft affectionate chriftian advice, and fuch folemn charges
relating to the performance of their duty
and the care of their fouls, as feemed plainly to intimate, that he apprehended it at
leaft very probable, he was taking his laft
farewel of them. There is great reafon to
believe, that he fpent the little remainder of
the time, which could not be much above
an hour, in thofe devout exercifes of foul,
which

* Several of thefe circumftances have fince been confirmed by the concurrent teftimony of another very credible perfon, Mr. Robert Douglafs, (now a furgeon in the
navy) who was a volunteer at Edinburgh juft before the
rebels entered the place ; who faw Colonel Gardiner come
from Haddington to the field of battle the day before the
action in a chaife, being (as from that circumftance he
fuppofed) in fo weak a ftate that he could not well endure
the fatigue of riding on horfeback. He obferved Colonel
Gardiner in difcourfe with feveral officers, the evening
before the engagement ; at which time it was afterwards
reported, he gave his advice to attack the rebels ; and
when it was overruled, he afterwards faw the Colonel
walk by himfelf in a very penfive manner.

which had fo long been habitual to him, and to which fo many circumftances did then concur to call him. The army was alarmed by break of day, by the noife of the rebels approach, and the attack was made before fun rife ; yet when it was light enough to difcern what paffed. As foon as the enemy came within gun fhot they made a furious fire ; and it is faid that the dragoons which conftituted the left wing, immediately fled. The Colonel, at the beginning of the onfet, which in the whole lafted but a few minutes, received a wound by a bullet in his left breaft, which made him give a fudden fpring in his faddle ; upon which his fervant, who had led the horfe, would have perfuaded him to retreat : But he faid it was only a wound in the flefh ; and fought on, though he prefently after received a fhot in his right thigh. In the mean time it was difcerned, that fome of the enemies fell by him ; and particularly one man, who had made him a treacherous vifit but a few days before, with great profeffions of zeal for the prefent eftablifhment.

Events of this kind pafs in lefs time than the defcription of them can be written, or than it can be read. The Colonel was for a few moments fupported by his men, and particularly by that worthy perfon Lieutenant

ant Colonel Whitney, who was ſhot through the arm here, and a few months after fell nobly in the battle of Falkirk; and by Lieutenant Weſt, a man of diſtinguiſhed bravery; as alſo by about fifteen dragoons, who ſtood by him to the laſt. But after a faint fire, the regiment in general was ſeized with a panic; and though their Colonel and ſome other gallant officers did what they could to rally them once or twice, they at laſt took a precipitate flight. And juſt in the moment when Colonel Gardiner ſeemed to be making a pauſe, to deliberate what duty required him to do in ſuch a circumſtance, an accident happened, which muſt, I think, in the judgment of every worthy and generous man, be allowed a ſufficient apology for expoſing his life to ſo great hazard, when his regiment had left him.*   He ſaw a party of the

* The Colonel, who was well acquainted with military hiſtory, might poſſibly remember, that in the battle at Blenheim, the illuſtrious Prince Eugene, when the horſe of the wing he commanded had run away thrice, charged at the head of the foot, and thereby greatly contributed to the glorious ſucceſs of the day. At leaſt ſuch an example may conduce to vindicate that noble ardour, which, amidſt all the applauſes of his country, ſome have been ſo cool and ſo critical as to blame. For my own part, I thank God that I am not called to apologize for his following his troops in their flight; which I fear would have been a much harder taſk; and which, dear as he was to me, would have grieved me much more than his death, with theſe heroic circumſtances attending it.

S

the foot, who were then bravely fighting near him, and whom he was ordered to fupport, had no officer to head them ; upon which he faid eagerly, in the hearing of the perfon from whom I had this account, " Thofe brave fellows would be cut to pieces " for want of a commander ;" or words to that effect : Which while he was fpeaking, he rode up to them, and cried out aloud, " Fire on, my lads, and fear nothing." But juft as the words were out of his mouth, an Highlander advanced towards him, with a fcythe faftened to a long pole, with which he gave him fuch a deep wound on his right arm, that his fword dropped out of his hand ; and at the fame time feveral others coming about him, while he was thus dreadfully entangled with that cruel weapon, he was dragged off from his horfe. The moment he fell, another Highlander, who, if the King's evidence at Carlifle may be credited, (as I know not why they fhould not, though the unhappy creature died denying it) was one Macnaught, who was executed about a year after, gave him a ftroke, either with a broad fword, or a Lochabar axe, (for my informant could not exactly diftinguifh) on the hinder part of his head, which was the mortal blow. All that his faithful attendant faw farther at this time was, that as his hat

was

was fallen off, he took it in his left hand,
and waved it as a signal to him to retreat;
and added, what were the last words he ever
heard him speak, " Take care of yourself :"
Upon which the servant retired.

It was reported at Edinburgh on the day
of the battle, by what seemed a considerable
authority, that as the Colonel lay in his
wounds, he said to a chief of the opposite
side, " You are fighting for an earthly
" crown, I am going to receive an heavenly
" one ;" or something to that purpose.
When I preached the sermon, long since
printed, on occasion of his death, I had great
reason to believe, that this report was true ;
though before the publication of it I began
to be in doubt : And on the whole, after
the most accurate inquiry I could possibly
make at this distance, I cannot get any convincing evidence of it. Yet I must here
observe, that it does not appear impossible,
that something of this kind might indeed be
uttered by him ; as his servant testifies, that
he spoke to him after receiving that fatal
blow, which would seem most likely to have
taken away the power of speech ; and as it
is certain he lived several hours after he fell.
If therefore any thing of this kind did happen, it must have been just about this in-
stant. But as to the story of his being taken
prisoner

prifoner and carried to the pretended Prince, (who by the way afterwards rode his horfe, and entered upon it into Derby) with feveral other circumftances which were grafted upon that interview, there is the moft undoubted evidence of its falfehood : For his attendant mentioned above affures me, that he himfelf immediately fled to a mill, at the diftance of about two miles from the fpot of ground on which the Colonel fell ; where he changed his drefs, and, difguifed like a miller's fervant, returned with a cart as foon as poffible ; which yet was not till near two hours after the engagement. The hurry of the action was then pretty well over, and he found his much honoured mafter, not only plundered of his watch and other things of value, but alfo ftripped of his upper garments and boots ; yet ftill breathing : And adds, that though he were not capable of fpeech, yet on taking him up he opened his eyes ; which makes it fomething queftionable, whether he were altogether infenfible. In this condition, and in this manner, he conveyed him to the church of Tranent, from whence he was immediately taken into the minifter's houfe, and laid in bed, where he continued breathing and frequently groaning, till about eleven in the forenoon ; when he took his final leave of pain and
                                                         forrow,

forrow, and undoubtedly rofe to thofe diftinguifhed glories which are referved for
thofe who have been fo eminently and remarkably *faithful unto death.*

From the moment in which he fell, it was
no longer a battle, but a rout and carnage.
The cruelties which the rebels (as it is generally faid,. under the command of Lord
Elcho) inflicted on fome of the King's troops
after they had afked quarter, are dreadfully
legible on the countenances of many who
furvived it.   They entered Colonel Gardiner's houfe, before he was carried off from
the field ; and, notwithftanding the ftrict
orders which the unhappy Duke of Perth
(whofe conduct is faid to have been very
humane in many inftances) gave to the contrary, every thing of value was plundered,
to the very curtains of the bed and hangings
of the rooms.   His papers were all thrown
into the wildeft diforder, and his houfe made
an hofpital, for the reception of thofe who
were wounded in the action.

Such was the clofe of a life, which had
been fo zealoufly devoted to God, and filled
up with fo many honourable fervices. This
was the death of him, who had been fo highly favoured by God, in the method by which
he was brought back to him after fo long and
fo great an eftrangement, and in the progrefs

S 2.   of

of so many years, during which (in the ex‑
preſſive phraſe of the moſt ancient of writers)
he had walked with him ;——to fall as God
threatened the people of his wrath that they
ſhould do, *with tumult, with ſhouting, and
with the ſound of the trumpet.* (Amos, ii. 2.)
Several other very worthy, and ſome of them
very eminent perſons, ſhared the ſame fate ;
either now in the battle of Preſton Pans, or
quickly after in that of Falkirk : Providence,.
no doubt, permitting it, to eſtabliſh our
faith in the rewards of an inviſible world ;
as well as to teach us, to ceaſe from man,
and fix our dependence on an almighty
arm.

The remains of this Chriſtian hero, (as I.
believe every reader is now convinced he
may juſtly be called) were interred the
Tueſday following, September 24, at the
pariſh church at Tranent, where he had uſ‑
ually attended divine ſervice, with great ſo‑
lemnity. His obſequies were honoured
with the preſence of ſome perſons of diſ‑
tinction, who were not afraid of paying that
laſt piece of reſpect to his memory, though
the country was then in the hands of the
enemy. But indeed there was no great
hazard in this ; for his character was ſo well
known, that even they themſelves ſpoke
honourably of him, and ſeemed to join with

his

his friends in lamenting the fall of fo brave and fo worthy a man.

The remoteſt poſterity will remember, for whom the honour of fubduing this unnatural and pernicious rebellion was referved ; and it will endear the perſon of the illuſtrious Duke of Cumberland, to all but the open or fecret abettors of it in the prefent age, and confecrate his name to immortal honours among all the friends of religion and liberty who ſhall arife after us. And I dare fay it will not be imagined that I at all derogate from his glory, in fuggefting, that the memory of that valinat and excellent perſon, whoſe memoirs I am now concluding, may in fome meafure have contributed to that fignal and complete victory, with which God was pleafed to crown the arms of his Royal Highnefs : For the force of fuch an example is very animating, and a painful confcioufnefs of having deferted fuch a commander in fuch extremity, muſt at leaſt awaken, where there was any ſpark of generofity, an earneſt defire to avenge his death on thofe who had facrificed his blood, and that of fo many other excellent perſons, to the views of their ambition, rapine, or bigotry.

The reflections I have made in my funeral fermon on my honoured friend, and in the
dedication

dedication of it to his worthy and moſt afflicted lady, ſuperſede many things which
might otherwiſe have properly been added
here. I conclude therefore with humbly
acknowledging the wiſdom and goodneſs of
that awful providence, which drew ſo thick
a gloom around him in the laſt hours of his
life, that the luſtre of his virtues might dart
through it with a more vivid and obſervable
ray. It is abundant matter of thankfulneſs,
that ſo ſignal a monument of grace, and ornament of the Chriſtian profeſſion, was raiſed in our age and country, and ſpared for ſo
many honourable and uſeful years. Nor
can all the tenderneſs of the moſt affectionate friendſhip, while its ſorrows bleed afreſh
in the view of ſo tragical a ſcene, prevent
my adoring the gracious appointment of the
great Lord of all events, that when the day
in which he muſt have expired without an
enemy, appeared ſo very near, the laſt ebb
of his generous blood ſhould be poured out,
as a kind of ſacred libation, to the liberties
of his country, and the honour of his God !
that all the other virtues of his character,
embalmed as it were by that precious ſtream,
might diffuſe around a more extenſive fra-
grancy, and be tranſmitted to the moſt re-
mote poſterity, with that peculiar charm
which they cannot but derive from their
                                    connection

connection with fo gallant a fall : An event (as that bleffed Apoftle, of whofe fpirit he fo deeply drank, has expreffed it) *according to his earneft expectation, and his hope, that in him Chrift might be glorified in all things, whether by his life, or by his death.*

APPENDIX.

APPENDIX.

Relating to the COLONEL's *Person.*

IN the midſt of ſo many more important articles, I had really forgot to ſay any thing of the perſon of Colonel GARDINER, of which neverthelefs it may be proper here to add a word or two. It was, as I am informed, in younger life, remarkably grace-ful and amiable : And I can eaſily believe it, from what I knew him to be, when our acquaintance began ; though he was then turned of fifty, and had gone through ſo many fatigues as well as dangers, which could not but leave ſome traces on his coun-tenance. He was tall, (I ſuppoſe ſomething more than ſix feet) well proportioned, and ſtrongly built : His eyes of a dark grey, and not very large ; his forehead pretty high ; his noſe of a length and height no way remarkable, but very well ſuited to his other features ; his cheeks not very prominent, his mouth moderately large, and his chin rather a little inclining (when I knew him) to be peaked. He had a ſtrong voice, and lively accent ; with an air very intrepid, yet attempered with much gentle-neſs : And there was ſomething in his manner of addreſs moſt perfectly eaſy and obliging, which was in a great meaſure the reſult of the great candour and benevolence of his natural temper ; and which, no doubt, was much improved by the deep humility which divine grace had wrought into his heart ; as-well as his having been accuſtomed from his early youth, to the company of perſons of diſtinguiſhed rank and polite behaviour.

VERSES.

VERSES

On the Death of Colonel GARDINER.

By the Rev. *Benjamin Sowden.*

Quis desiderio sit pudor, aut modus,
Tam chari capitis?   HOR.

COULD piety perpetuate human breath,
     Or shield one mortal from the shafts of death,
Thou ne'er, illustrious man! thou ne'er hadst been
A palid corpse on Preston's fatal plain.
Or could her hand, though impotent to save
Consummate worth, redeem it from the grave,
Soon would thy urn resign its sacred trust,
And recent life reanimate thy dust.

     But vain the wish.—The savage hand of war—
Oh how shall words the mournful tale declare!
Too soon the news afflicted friendship hears,
Too soon, alas! confirm'd her boding fears.

     Struck with the sound, unconscious of redress,
She felt thy wounds, and wept severe distress.
A while dissolv'd in trucelefs grief she lay,
Which left thee to relentless rage a prey.

     At length kind Fame suspends our heaving sighs,
And wipes the sorrows from our flowing eyes;
Gives us to know, thine exit well supply'd
Those blooming laurels victory deny'd.
When thy great soul supprefs'd each timid moan,
And soar'd triumphant in a dying groan,   [plaint,
Thy fall, which rais'd, now calms each wild com-
Thy fall, which join'd the *hero* to the *faint.*

                                        As

As o'er th' expiring lamp the quiv'ring flame
Collects its luftre in a brighter gleam,
Thy virtues, glimm'ring on the verge of night,
Through the dim fhade diffus'd celeftial light;
A radiance, death or time can ne'er deftroy,
Th' aufpicious omen of eternal joy.

Hence ev'ry unavailing grief! No more
As haplefs thy removal we deplore.
Thy gufhing veins, in ev'ry drop they bleed,
Of patriot warriors fhed the fruitful feed.
Soon fhall the ripen'd harveft rife in arms
To crufh rebellion's infolent alarms.
While profp'rous moments footh'd thro' life his way,
Conceal'd from public view the hero lay:
But when affliction clouded his decline,
It not eclips'd, but made his honours fhine;
Gave them to beam confpicuous from the gloom,
And plant unfading trophies round his tomb.

So ftars are loft, amidft the blaze of day:
But when the fun withdraws his golden ray,
Refulgent thro' th' etherial arch they roll,
And gild the wide expanfe from pole to pole.

A SERMON,

The Christian Warrior animated and crowned :

A

S E R M O N,

OCCASIONED BY THE

HEROICK DEATH

OF THE

Hon. Col. JAMES GARDINER,

WHO WAS SLAIN IN THE

BATTLE at *PRESTON PANS,*

SEPTEMBER 21, 1745.

PREACHED at NORTHAMPTON, October 13,
BY P. DODDRIDGE, D. D.

—————————Ille Timorum
Maximus haud urget Lethi Metus :———
———— Ignavum Redituræ parcere Vitæ.

LUCAN.

PRINTED AT *BOSTON,*
BY I. THOMAS AND E. T. ANDREWS,
FAUST's STATUE, No. 45, *Newbury Street.*
MDCCXCII.

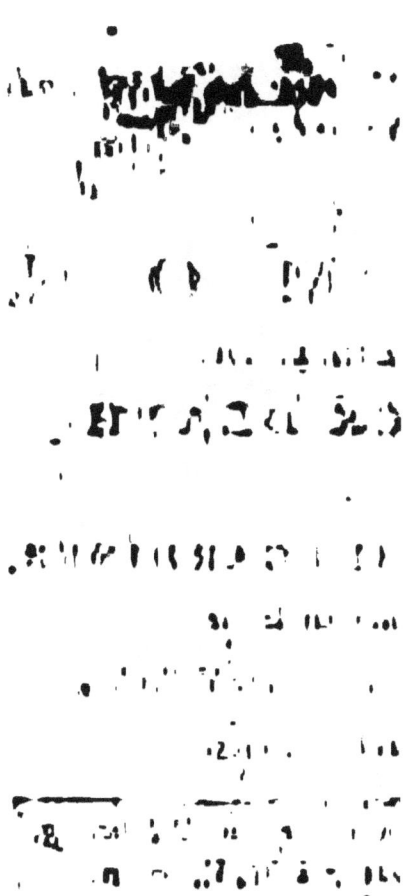

Lady Frances Gardiner.

MADAM,

THE intimate knowledge I had of Col. Gardiner's private as well as publick character, and of that endeared friendship which so long subsisted between him and your ladyship, makes me more sensible than most others can be, both of the inexpressible loss you have sustained, and of the exquisite sense you have of it. I might, in some degree, argue what you felt, from the agony with which my own heart was torn by that ever to be lamented stroke, which deprived the nation, and the church, of so great an ornament and blessing: And indeed, Madam, I was so sensible of your calamity, as to be ready in my first thoughts to congratulate you, when I heard the report which at first prevailed, that you died under the shock. Yet cooler reflection teaches me, on many accounts, to rejoice that your ladyship has survived that dearest part of yourself; though after having been so lovely and pleasant in your lives, it would have been matter of personal rejoicing, in death not to have been divided. The numerous and promising offspring with which God hath blessed your marriage, had evidently the

highest

higheſt intereſt in the continued life of ſo pious
and affectionate a mother: And I hope, and aſſuredly believe, there was a' more important, and
to you a much dearer intereſt concerned, as God
may be, and is, fignally honoured, by the manner
in which you bear this heavieſt and moſt terrible
ſtroke of his paternal rod.

God had been pleaſed, Madam, to make you
both eminent for a variety of graces; and he has
proportionably diſtinguiſhed you both, in the opportunity he has given you of exerciſing thoſe,
which ſuit the moſt painful ſcenes, that can attend
a pious and an honourable life. But when I conſider what it is, to have loſt ſuch a man, at ſuch
time, and in ſuch circumſtances, I muſt needs declare, that brave and heroick as the death of the
Colonel was, your ladyſhip's part is beyond all
compariſon the hardeſt. Yet even here has the
grace of Chriſt been ſufficient for you; and I join
with your ladyſhip in adoring the power and
faithfulneſs of him, who has here ſo remarkably
ſhewn, that he forgets not his promiſe to all his
people, of a ſtrength proportionable to their day;
that they may be enabled to glorify him in the
hotteſt furnace, into which it is poſſible they
ſhould be caſt.

To hear, (as I have heard from ſeveral perſons
of diſtinguiſhed character, who have lately had
the happineſs of being near your ladyſhip) of that
meek

meek refignation to the divine will, of that calm
patience, of that Chriftian courage, with which,
in fo weak a ftate of health and fpirits, you have
fupported under this awful providence, has given
me great pleafure, but no furprife. So near a relation to fo brave a man might have taught fome
degree of fortitude, to a foul lefs fufceptible of it
than your ladyfhip's. Nor is there any doubt but
that the prayers he has fo long been laying up in
ftore for you, efpecially fince the decay of his conftitution gave him reafon to expect a fpeedy remove, will affuredly at fuch a feafon come into
remembrance before God. And above all, the
fublime principles of the Chriftian religion, fo
deeply imbibed into your own heart as well as
his, will not fail to exert their energy on fuch an
occafion. Thefe, Madam, will teach you to view
the hand of a wife, a righteous, and a gracious
God in this event ; and will fhew you, that a
friendfhip founded on fuch a bafis, fo very in-
dearing, and fo clofely cemented, as that which
has been here for many years a bleffing to you
both, can know only a very fhort interruption,
and will foon grow up into a union infinitely
nobler and more delightful, which never fhall be
liable to any feparation. .

In the mean time, Madam, it may comfort us
not a little under the fenfe of our prefent lofs, to
think what religious improvement we may gain by
it, if we are not wanting to ourfelves : And happy

shall we be indeed, if we so hear the rod, as to receive the instructions it so naturally suggests and inforces. Persons of any serious reflection will learn from this awful event, how little we can judge of the divine favour by the visible dispensations of Providence here : They will learn, (and it may be of great importance to consider it, just in such a crisis as this) that no distinguished degree of piety can secure the very best of men from the sword of a common enemy : And they will see (written, alas, in characters of the most precious blood, that war ever spilt in our island) the vanity of the surest protectors and comforters which mortality can afford, at a time when they are most needed.

These are general instructions, which I hope thousands will receive, on this universally lamented occasion : But to you, Madam, and to me, and to all that were honoured with the most intimate friendship of this Christian hero, his death has a peculiar voice. Whilst it leads us back into so many past scenes of delight, in the remembrance of which we now pour out our souls within us, it calls aloud, amidst all this tender distress, for a tribute of humble thankfulness to God, that ever we enjoyed such a friend, and especially in such an intimacy of mutual affection ; and that we had an opportunity of observing, in so many instances, the secret recesses of a heart, which God had enriched, adorned, and ennobled with so much of

his

his own image, and such abundant communica-
tions of his grace : It calls for our redoubled diligence and resolution, in imitating that bright af-
semblage of virtues, which shone so resplendent
in our illustrious friend : And surely it must, by
a kind of irresistible influence, mortify our affections to this impoverished world ; and must cause
nature to concur with grace, in raising our hearts
upwards to that glorious world, where he dwells
triumphant and immortal, and waits our arrival
with an ardour of pure and elevated love, which
it was impossible for death to quench.

Next to these views, nothing can give your
ladyship greater satisfaction, than to reflect, how
happy you made the amiable consort you have
lost, in that intimate relation you so long bore to
each other ; in which, I well know, that growing years ripened and increased your mutual esteem and friendship. Nor will your generous
heart be insensible of that pleasure, which may a-
rise from reflecting, that the manner of his death
(though in itself so terrible, that we dare not trust
imagination with the particular review) was to
him, in those circumstances, most glorious, to religion highly ornamental, and to his country, great
as its loss is, on various accounts beneficial. For
very far be it from us to think, that Colonel
Gardiner, though fallen by the weapons of rebellion and treason, has fought and died in vain. I
trust in God, that so heroick a behaviour will inspire

spire our warriors with augmented courage, now
they are called to exert it in a cause, the most noble and important that can ever be in question,
the cause of our laws, our liberty, and religion.
I trust, that all who keep up a correspondence
with heaven by prayer, will renew their interces-
sion for this bleeding land with increasing fervour, now we have lost one who stood in the
breach with such unwearied importunity. And
I am well assured, that of the multitudes who lay
up his memory in their inmost hearts with veneration and love, not a few will be often joining
their most affectionate prayers to God, for your
ladyship, and the dear rising branches of your
family, with those which you may, in consequence
of a thousand obligations, always expect from

Madam,

Your ladyship's most faithful

and obedient humble servant,

P. DODDRIDGE.

Northampton, Nov. 27, 1745.

A

S E R M O N.

REV. II. 10. *latter part.*

——BE THOU FAITHFUL UNTO DEATH, AND I WILL GIVE THEE A CROWN OF LIFE.

IT is a glory peculiar to the Chriſtian religion, that it is capable of yielding joy
and triumph to the mind, amidſt calamities,
in which the ſtrength of nature, and of a
philoſophy that has no higher a ſupport,
can hardly give it ſerenity, or even patience.
Thoſe boaſted aids are but like a candle in
ſome tempeſtuous night, which how artiſic-
ially ſoever it may be fenced in, is often ex-
tinguiſhed amidſt the ſtorm, in which it
ſhould guide and cheer the traveller, or the
mariner; whom it leaves on a ſudden, in,
darkneſs, horror, and fear: While the conſolation of the goſpel, like the ſun, makes a
ſure day even when behind the thickeſt
clould

cloud, and foon emerges from it with an acceffion of more fenfible luftre.

The obfervation is verified in thefe words, confidered in connection with that awful providence, which has this day determined my thoughts to fix upon them, as the fubject of my difcourfe; the fall of that truly great and good man, Colonel GARDINER: The endearing tendernefs of whofe friendfhip would have rendered his death an unfpeakable calamity to me, had his character been only of the common ftandard; as on the other hand, the exalted excellency of his character makes his death to be lamented by thoufands, who were not happy in any peculiar intimacy or perfonal acquaintance with him.

While we mourn the brave warrior, the exemplary Chriftian, and the affectionate friend; loft to ourfelves and our country, to the church and the world, at a time when we moft needed all the defence of his bravery, all the edification of his example, all the comfort of his converfe: Struck with the various and aggravated forrow of fo fudden, and fo terrible a blow, methinks there is but one voice that can cheer us, which is this of the great captain of our falvation, fo lately addreffing him, and ftill addreffing us, in thefe comprehenfive and animated words:

Be

Be thou faithful unto death, and I will give thee a crown of life.

With regard to the connection of them, it may be sufficient to observe, that our Lord, in all these seven epistles to the Asiatick churches, represents the Christian life as a warfare, and the blessings of the future state as rewards to be bestowed on conquerors. To him that overcometh, will I give such and such royal donatives. Pursuing the same allegory, he warns the church of Smyrna of an approaching combat, which should be attended with some severe circumstances. Some of them were to become captives; the Devil shall cast some of you into prison: And though the power of the enemy was to be limited, in its extent as well as its duration, to the tribulation of ten days, it seems to be implied, that while many were harrassed and distressed during that time, some of them should before the close of it be called to resist unto blood. But their great leader furnishes them with suitable armour, and proportionable courage, by this gracious assurance, which it is our present business farther to contemplate: Be thou faithful unto death, and I will give thee a crown of life.

In which words you naturally observe a charge—and a promise by which it is inforced.

forced. I fhall briefly illuftrate each, and
then conclude with fome reflections upon
the whole.

Firft, I am to open the charge here given:
Be thou faithful unto death.

Concerning which I would obferve, that
though it is immediately addreffed to the
church at Smyrna, yet the nature of the
thing, and numberlefs paffages of the divine
word concur to prove, that it is common in
its obligation, to all Chriftians, and indeed
to all men.

I fhall not be large in explaining the nature of faithfulnefs in general ; concerning
which I might fhew you, that the word here
rendered faithful, has fometimes a relation
to the teftimony which God has given us,
and fometimes to fome truft that he has re-
pofed in us. In the former fenfe, it is
properly rendered believing, and oppofed to
infidelity : Be not faithlefs, but believing.*
In the latter, it is oppofed to injuftice : He
that is faithful in that which is leaft, is faithful alfo in much ; whereas he that is unjuft
in the leaft, is unjuft alfo in much.† And
it is in reference to this fenfe of it, that our
Lord reprefents himfelf, as faying to the
man who had improved his talents aright,
well done, good and faithful fervant.‡ Our
deceafed

* John xx. 27.   † Luke xvi. 10.   ‡ Mat. xxv. 23.

deceafed friend was fo remarkably faithful in both thefe fenfes ; fo ready to admit, and fo zealous to defend the faith once delivered to the faints.; and fo active in improving thofe various talents, with which, in mercy to many others as well as to himfelf, God had intrufted him ; that it was very natural to touch upon thefe fignifications of the word, though it has here a more particular view to another virtue, for which he was fo illuftrioufly confpicuous, I mean, the couragious fidelity of a foldier in his warfare.

In this fenfe of the word, it is oppofed to treachery or cowardice, defertion or difobedience to military orders. And thus it is ufed elfewhere in this fame book of the Revelation, when fpeaking of thofe who war under the banner of the lamb, the King of Kings, and Lord of Lords, the infpired writer tells us, they are called, and chofen, and faithful,* a felect body of brave and valiant foldiers.

This hint will alfo fix the eafieft and plaineft fenfe, in which the perfons, to whom the text is addreffed, are required to be faithful unto death : Which, though it does indeed in general imply, a patient continuance in well doing,† in whatever fcenes

of

* Rev. xvii. 14.   † Rom. ii. 7.

.U   ɪ

of life divine providence may place us; yet does especially refer to martial bravery, and exprefs a readinefs to face death in its moft terrible forms, when our great General fhall lead us on to it. You well know this to be an indifpenfable condition of our being acknowledged by him in the day of his final triumph: And of this he warned thofe that gathered around him, when he was firft raifing his army, under the greateft difadvantages in outward appearance; exprefsly and plainly telling them, that they muft be content to follow him to martyrdom, to follow him to crucifixion, when they receive the word of command to do it; or that all their profeffion of regard to him would be in vain. If any man, fays he, will come after me, let him deny himfelf, and take up his crofs, and follow me:* For he that loveth his own life more than me, is not worthy of me;† he does not deferve the honour of bearing my name, and paffing for one of my foldiers; indeed he cannot on any terms be my difciple.‡

This therefore is in effect the language of our Lord, when he fays, be thou faithful unto death: It is as if he had faid, " Re-" member all you of Smyrna, or of any oth-" er place and country, that call yourfelves
" Chriftians,

* Mark, viii. 34. † Mat. x. 37, 39. ‡ Luke, xiv. 26.

" Chriſtians, thoughout all generations, that
" you were by baptiſm inliſted under my
" banners : Remember, that you have as it
" were ſealed, and ſubſcribed your engage-
" ment to me, by every ſacrament you have
" ſince attended ;" (as indeed it is well
known, the word *ſacrament* originally ſigni-
fies a military oath, which ſoldiers took as a
pledge of fidelity to their General :) " Re-
" member, therefore, that you are ever to
" continue with me, and to march forward
" under my direction, whatever hardſhips
" and fatigues may lie in the way. And
" remember, that if I lead you on to the
" moſt formidable combat, you muſt cheer-
" fully obey the word of command, and
" charge boldly, though you ſhould imme-
" diately die, whether by the ſword, or by
" fire. Should you dare to flee, I am my-
" ſelf your enemy ; and the weapons which
" I bear, would juſtly be levelled at your
" own traiterous heads. But if you bravely
" follow me, I know how to make you am-
" ple amends, even though you fall in the
" action. When no human power and
" gratitude can reach you, it is my glorious
" prerogative to engage, that to thoſe who
" are thus faithful unto death, I will give a
" crown of life." We are therefore,

Secondly,

: Secondly, To consider the promise, by which the charge is enforced : I will give thee a crown of life.

And here I might observe, a crown of life is the glorious reward proposed, and it is to be received from the hand of Christ.

- 1. A crown of life is the reward proposed : Which we are sure in this connection implies, both grandeur and felicity ; here, though rarely, connected together.

There is, no doubt, an allusion in these words, to the ancient, and I think very prudent, custom of animating the bravery of soldiers by honorary rewards, and particularly by crowns ; sometimes of laurel, and sometimes, more rarely, of silver and gold ; which they were permitted to wear on publick occasions, and in consequence of receiving which they were sometimes intitled to some peculiar immunities. But here our Lord Jesus Christ, conscious of his own divine power and prerogative, speaks with a dignity and elevation, which no earthly prince or commander could ever assume ; promising a crown of life, and that, as was observed before, even to those who should fall in the battle ; A crown of life in the highest sense ; not only one, which should ever be fresh and fair, but which should give immortality to the happy brow it adorned ;

and

and be forever worn, not only as the monument of bravery and victory, but as the ensign of royalty too : A crown connected with a kingdom, and with what no other kingdom can give, perpetual life to enjoy it ; perpetual youth, and vigour to relish all its delights. And this is agreeable to the language of other scriptures, where we read of the crown of life, which the Lord hath promised to them that love him ;* a crown of righteousnefs, which the Lord the righteous Judge shall give ;† a crown of glory, which fadeth not away.‡ We may also observe,

2. That it is said to be given by Christ.

This some pious commentators have explained, as intimating, that it is the gift of the Redeemer's free and unmerited grace, and not a retribution due to the merit of him that receiveth it. And this is an undoubted truth, which it is of the highest importance to acknowledge and confider. The proper wages of sin is death ; but eternal life is (in oppofition to wages) the gift of God through Jefus Chrift our Lord.§ We should humbly own it every day, that there is no proportion between the value of

our

* Jam. i. 12.   † 2 Tim. iv. 8.   ‡ 1 Pet. v. 4.
§ Rom. vi. 23.

our fervices, and the crown which we expect
to receive : Should own that it is mercy
that pardons our fins, and grace that accepts
our fervices ; much more, that crowns them.
Grace, grace, fhall (as it were) be engraven
upon that crown, in characters large and
indelible : Nor will that infcription diminifh
its luftre, or impair the pleafure with which
we fhall receive it. I could not forbear
mentioning this thought, as a truth of the
utmoft importance, which ftands on the
firmeft bafis of very many exprefs fcriptures';
a truth, of which perhaps no man living had
ever a deeper fenfe, than our deceafed friend.
But I mention it thus obliquely, becaufe it
may be doubted whether we can juftly argue
it from hence ; fince the word *give* is fometimes ufed for rendering a retribution juftly
due, and that in inftances where grace and
favour have, in propriety of fpeech, no
concern at all.*

But it is certain that this expreffion, I will
give thee a crown of life, is intended to lead
our thoughts to this important circumftance ;
that this crown is to be received from the
hand of Chrift himfelf. And the Apoftle
Paul evidently refers to the fame circumftance,

* Compare Mat. xx. 8. Give the labourers their hire.
Col. iv. 1. Mafters, give unto your fervants that which
is juft and equal.

ſtance, in terms which ſhew how much he entered into the ſpirit of the thought, when he ſays, the Lord the righteous judge ſhall give it me :* He himſelf, the great judge of the conteſt, whoſe eye witneſſes the whole courſe of it, whoſe deciſion cannot err, and from whoſe ſentence there is no appeal: Alluding to the judge who preſided in the Grecian games, who was always a perſon of rank and eminence, and himſelf reached forth the reward to him who overcame in them.

So that on the whole, when our Lord Jeſus Chriſt ſays, be thou faithful unto death, and I will give thee a crown of life ; methinks our devout meditations may expatiate upon the words, in ſome ſuch paraphraſe as this. It is as if he had ſaid, to you, and to me, and to all his people; " Oh my faithful ſoldiers, " fear not death in its moſt terrible array, " for you are immortal. Fear not them " that can kill the body :† You have a no- " bler part, which they cannot reach ; and I " will undertake, not only for its reſcue; but " its happineſs. I will anſwer for it, on the " honour of my royal word, that it ſhall live " in a ſtate of noble enlargement, of tri- " umphant joy. Think on me : I am he " that liveth, though I was dead ; and be- "hold,

---

* 2 Tim. iv. 8.   † Mat. x. 28.

" hold, I am alive for ever more:* And be-
" caufe I live, you fhall live alfo;† fhall
" exift in a ftate, that deferves the great and
" honourable name of life ; fo that earth in
" all its luftre and pleafure, when compared
" with it, is but a fcene of death, or at beft
" as an amufing dream when one awaketh."‡

We may alfo confider him, as purfuing
this animating addrefs, and faying, " My
" brave companions in tribulation and pa-
" tience, you fhall not only live, but reign.
" Think not, thou good foldier, who art now
" fighting under my banner, that thy Gen-
" eral will wear his honours alone. If I
" have my crown, if I have my triumph, be
" affured that thou alfo fhalt have thine.
" Thou mayeft indeed feem to perifh in the
" combat, and thy friends may mourn, and
" thine enemies infult, as if thou wert ut-
" terly cut off. But behold, true victory
" fpreads over thee her golden wing, and
" holds out, not a garland of fading flowers
" or leaves, but a crown that fhall keep its
" luftre, when all the coftlieft gems on earth
" are melted in the general burning ; yea,
" when the luminaries of heaven are extin-
" guifhed, and the fun and ftars fade away
" in their orbs."

" Nor

---

* Rev. i, 18.   † John, xiv. 19.   ‡ Pfal. lxxiii. 20.

" Nor will I," does he feem to fay, " fend
" thee this crown by fome inferior hand;
" not even by the nobleft angel, that waits
" on the throne I have now afcended.
" Thou fhalt receive it from mine own
" hand ;" (from that hand, which would
make the leaft gift valuable : What a dignity then will it add to the greateft !) " Nor
" will I myfelf confer this reward in private ;
" it fhall be given with the moft magnificent
" folemnity. Thou fhalt be brought to me
" before the affembled world : Thy name
" fhall be called over ; thou fhalt appear,
" and I will own thee, and crown thee, in
" publick view. Thy friends fhall fee it
" with raptures of joy, and congratulate an
" honour in which they fhall alfo fhare.
" Thine enemies fhall fee it with envy and
" with rage, to increafe their confufion and
" mifery : They fhall fee, that while by their
" malicious affaults they were endeavouring
" to deftroy thee, they were only eftablifhing
" thy throne, and brightening the luftre,
" which fhall forever adorn thy brow ; while
" theirs is blafted with the thunder of refift-
" lefs wrath, and deep engraven with the
" indelible marks of vengeance. This crown
" fhalt thou forever wear, as the perpetual
" token of my efteem and affection : Nor
" fhall it be merely a fhining ornament : A
" rich

" rich revenue, a glorious authority, goes
" along with it. Thou fhalt reign forever
" and ever ;* and be a king, as well as a
" prieft, unto God."†

They who enter by a lively faith into the
import of thefe glorious words, will (I doubt
not) pardon my having expatiated fo largely
upon them. We have believed, and therefore have we fpoken :‡ And I queftion not,
but that many of you have, in the courfe of
this reprefentation, prevented me in fome
of the refleƈtions, which naturally arife from
fuch a fubjeƈt. Yet it may not be improper
to affift your devout meditations upon them.

1. What reafon have we to adore the
grace of our bleffed Redeemer, which pre-
pares, and beftows, fuch rewards as thefe !

While we hear him faying, be thou faithful unto death, and I will give thee a crown
of life ; methinks it is but natural for each
of our hearts to anfwer, " Lord, doft thou
" fpeak of giving a crown, a crown of life
" and glory to me ! Too great, too great,
" might the favour feem, if I, who have fo
" often lifted up my rebellious hand againft
" thy throne, might be allowed to lay down
" this guilty head in the duft, and lofe the
" memory of my treafons, and the fenfe of
" my punifhment together, in everlafting
　　　　　　　　　　　forgetfulnefs.

* Rev. xxii. 5.　† Rev. i. 6.　‡ 2 Cor. iv. 13.

" forgetfulnefs. And is fuch a crown pre-
" pared, and wilt thou, my injured fovereign,
" who mighteft fo juftly arm thyfelf with
" vengeance againft me, beftow this crown
" with thine own hand ; with all thefe other
" circumftances of dignity, fo as even to
" make my triumphs thine own !——What
" is my ftricteft fidelity to thee ? Though I
" do indeed (as I humbly defire that I may)
" continue faithful unto death, I am yet but
" an unprofitable fervant ; I have done no
" more than my duty.* I have purfued
" thy work, in thy ftrength ; and, in confe-
" quence of that love which thou haft put
" into my heart, it hath been its own reward :
" And doft thou thus crown one favour with
" another !——Bleffed Jefus, I would with
" all humility lay that crown at thy feet,
" acknowledging before thee, and the whole
" world, (as I fhall at length do in a more
" expreffive form) that it is not only the gift
" of thy love, but the purchafe of thy blood.
" Never, never had I beheld it, otherwife
" than at an unapproachable diftance, as an
" aggravation of my mifery and defpair,
" hadft not thou worn another crown, a
" crown of infamy and of thorns. The
" gems which muft forever adorn my tem-
" ples, were formed from thofe precious
                                    " drops

* Luke, xvii. 10.

" drops, that once trickled down thine; and
. " all the fplendor of my robes of triumph is
" owing to their being wafhed in the blood
" of the lamb."* With what pleafing
wonder may we purfue the thought ! And
while it employs our mind,

2. How juftly may this awaken a generous ambition to fecure this crown to ourfelves !

Dearly as it was purchafed by our blelfed
Redeemer, it is moft freely offered to us, to
the youngeft, to the, meaneft, to the moft
unworthy. It is not prepared, merely for
thofe that have worn an earthly diadem or
coronet : (Would to God it were not defpifed by moft of them, as a thing lefs worthy of their thoughts, than the moft trifling
amufement, by which they unbend their
minds from the weighty cares attending their
ftation !) But it is prepared for you, and for
you ; even for every one, who thinks it
worth purfuing, and accepting, upon the
terms of the gofpel covenant ; for every
one, who believing in Chrift, and loving
him, is humbly determined through his
grace to be faithful unto death. And fhall
this glorious propofal be made to you in
vain ? Were it an earthly crown that could
lawfully be obtained, are there not many of
us,

* Rev. vii. 14.

us, notwithſtanding all its weight of anxie-
ties, and all the piercing thorns with which.
we might know it to be lined, that would
be ready eagerly to ſeize it, and perhaps to
contend and quarrel with each other for it ?
But here is no foundation for contention.
Here is a crown for each ; and ſuch a crown,
that all the royal ornaments of all the
princes upon earth, when compared with it,
are lighter than a feather, and viler than
duſt. And ſhall we neglect it ? Shall we
refuſe it, from ſuch a hand too, as that by
which it is offered ? Shall we ſo judge ourſelves unworthy of eternal life,* as thereby
indeed to make ourſelves worthy of eternal
death ? For there is no other alternative.—
But bleſſed be God, it is not univerſally
neglected. There are, I doubt not, among
you, many who purſue it, many who ſhall
aſſuredly obtain it. For their ſakes let us
reflect,

3. How courageouſly may the heads
which are to wear ſuch a crown, be lifted up
to face all the trials of life and death !

Thoſe trials may be various, and perhaps
extreme ; but if borne aright, far from de-
priving us of this crown, they will only ſerve
to increaſe its luſtre. It is the apoſtle Paul's
expreſs aſſertion ; and he ſpeaks, as tranſ-

W

ported

* Acts, xiii. 46.

ported with the thought : For this caufe we faint not, but though the outward man per-iſh, yet the inward man is renewed day by day : For our light affliction, which is but for a moment, worketh for us a far more exceeding and eternal weight of glory ; while we look not at the things which are feen, but at the things which are not feen ; for the things which are feen are temporal, but the things which are not feen are eter-nal.* Surely with this fupport, we may not only live, but triumph, in poverty, in reproach, in weakneſs, in pain : And with this we may die, not only ferenely, but joyfully. Oh my friends, where are our hearts ? Where is our faith ? Nay, I will add, where is our reafon ? Why are not our eyes, our defires, and our hopes, more fre-quently directed upward ? Surely one ray from that refplendent diadem might be fuf-ficient to confound all the falfe charms of thefe tranfitory vanities, which indeed owe all their luftre to the darkneſs in which they are placed. Surely when our fpirits are overwhelmed within us, one glance of it might be fufficient to animate and elevate, and might teach us to fay, in the midft of dangers, forrows, and death, in all thefe things we are more than conquerors, through
him

---

* 2 Cor. iv. 16, 17, 18.

him that loved us.* Thus have some triumphed in the last extremities of nature; and both the subject, and the occasion also, loudly calls us to reflect,

4. What reason we have to congratulate those happy souls, that have already received the crown of life !

When we are weeping over the cold, yea the bleeding remains of such, surely it is for ourselves, and not for them, that the stream flows. The thought of their condition, far from moving our compassion, may rather inspire us with joy, and with praise. Look not on their pale countenance, nor on the wide and deep wounds, through which perhaps the soul rushed out to seize the great prize of its faith and hope; though even those wounds appear beautiful, when earned by distinguished virtue, by piety to their country, and their God. Look not on the eyes closed in death, or the once honoured and beloved head, now covered with the dust of the grave : But view, by an internal believing eye, that different form which the exalted triumphant spirit already wears, the earnest of a yet brighter glory. Their great leader, whose care of them we are fondly ready to suspect, or secretly to complain of as deficient in such circumstances

as

* Rom. viii. 37.

as thefe, points, as it were, to the white
robes, and the flourifhing palms, which he
has given them ; and calls for our regard to
the crowns of life, which he has fet on their
heads, and to the fongs of joy and praife to
which he has formed their exulting tongues.
And do we fully and difhonor their triumphs
with our tears ? Do we think fo meanly of
heaven, and of them, as to wifh them with us
again ; that they might eat and drink at our
tables ; that they might talk with us in our
low language ; that they might travel with us
from ftage to ftage in this wildernefs ; and
take their fhare with us in thofe vanities of
life, of which we ourfelves are fo often
weary, that there is hardly a week, or a day,
in which we are not lifting up our eyes, and
faying with a deep inward groan, oh that we
had wings like a dove ! Then would we flee
away, and be at reft.*

Surely, with relation to thefe faithful foldiers of Jefus Chrift, who have already fall-
en, it is matter of no fmall joy to reflect,
that their warfare is accomplifhed ;† that
they have at length paffed through every
fcene in which their fidelity could be en-
dangered ; fo that now, they are inviolably
fecure. How much more then fhould we
rejoice, that they are entered, not only into
the reft, but into the joy of their Lord ; that

* Pfal. lv. 6.   † Ifai. xl. 2.   they

they conquered, even when they fell, and are now reaping the fruits, the celeſtial and immortal fruits, of that laſt great victory?

A ſenſe of honour often taught the heathens, when attending thoſe friends to the funeral pile who had died honourably in their country's cauſe, to uſe ſome ceremonies expreſſive of their joy for their glory; though that glory was an empty name, and all the reward of it a wreath of laurel, which was ſoon to crackle in the flame, and vaniſh into ſmoak. And ſhall not the joy and glory of the living ſpirit affect us, much more than they could be affected with the honours paid to the mangled corpſe?

Let us then think with reverence, and with joy, on the pious dead; and eſpecially on thoſe, whom God honoured with any ſpecial opportunities of approving their fidelity, in life, or in death: And if we mourn, (as who, in ſome circumſtances, can forbear it?) let it be as Chriſtians with that mixture of high congratulation, with that erect countenance, and that undaunted heart, which becomes thoſe that ſee by faith their exaltation and felicity; and burning with a ſtrong and ſacred eagerneſs to join their triumphant company, let us be ready to ſhare in the moſt painful of their trials, that we may alſo ſhare in their glories.

And

And furely, if I have ever known a life, and a death, capable of infpiring us with thefe fentiments in their fublimeft elevations, it was the life and the death of that illuftrious Chriftian hero, Col. Gardiner; whofe character was too well known to many of you, by fome months refidence here, to need your being informed of it from me; and whofe hiftory was too remarkable, to be confined within thofe few remaining moments, which muft be allotted to the finifhing of this difcourfe. Yet there was fomething fo uncommon in both, that I think it of high importance to the honour of the gofpel and grace of Chrift, that they fhould be delivered down to pofterity, in a diftinct and particular view. And therefore, as the providence of God, in concurrence with that moft intimate and familiar friendfhip with which this great and good man was pleafed to honour me, gives me an opportunity of fpeaking of many important things, efpecially relating to his religious experiences, with greater exactnefs and certainty than moft others might be capable of doing; and as he gave me his full permiffion, in cafe I fhould have the affliction to furvive him, to declare freely whatever I knew of him, which I might apprehend conducive to the glory of God, and the advancement of religion;

ligion; I purpofe publifhing, in a diftinct
tract, fome remarkable paffages of his life,
illuftrated by extracts from his own letters,
which fpeak in the moft forcible manner the
genuine fentiments of his heart.. But as I
promife myfelf confiderable affiftance in this
work from fome valuable perfons in the
northern part of our ifland, and poffibly
from fome of his own papers, to which our
prefent confufions forbid my accefs, I muft
delay the execution of this defign at leaft
for a few months ; and muft likewife take
heed, that I do not too much anticipate what
I may then offer to the publick view, by
what it might otherwife be very proper to
mention now.

Let it therefore fuffice for the prefent to
remind you, that Colonel Gardiner was one
of the moft illuftrious inftances of the energy, and indeed I muft alfo add, of the
fovereignty of divine grace, which I have
heard or read of in modern hiftory. He
was in the moft amazing and miraculous
manner, without any divine ordinance, without any religious opportunity, or peculiar
advantage, deliverance, or affliction, reclaimed on a fudden, in the vigour of life and
health, from the moft licentious and abandoned fenfuality, not only to a fteady courfe
of regularity and virtue, but to high devotion,

tion, and ſtrict, though unaffected ſanctity of manners : A courſe, (in which he perſiſted for more than twenty ſix years, that is, to the cloſe of life) ſo remarkably eminent for piety towards God, diffuſive humanity and Chriſtian charity, lively faith, deep humility, ſtrict temperance, active diligence in improving time, meek reſignation to the will of God, ſteady patience in enduring afflictions, unaffected contempt of ſecular intereſt, and reſolute and couragious zeal in maintaining truth, as well as in reproving and (where his authority might take place) reſtraining vice and wickedneſs of every kind ; that I muſt deliberately declare, that when I conſider all theſe particulars together, it is hard to ſay where, but in the book of God, he found his example, or where he has left his equal. Every one of theſe articles, with many more, I hope, if God ſpare my life, to have an opportunity of illuſtrating, in ſuch a manner as to ſhew, that he was a living demonſtration of the energy and ex-cellency of the Chriſtian religion ; nor can I imagine how I can ſerve its intereſts bet-ter, than by recording what I have ſeen and known upon this head, known to my own edification, as well as my joy.

But oh, how ſhall I lead back your thoughts, and my own, to what we once

enjoyed

enjoyed in him, without too deep and tender a fenfe of what we have loft ! To have
poured out his foul in blood ; to have fallen
by the favage and rebellious hands of his
own countrymen, at the wall of his own
houfe ; deferted by thofe, who were under
the higheft obligations that can be imagined
to have defended his life with their own ;
and above all, to have feen with his dying
eyes the enemies of our religion and liberties triumphant, and to have heard in his
lateft moments the horrid noife of their in-
fulting fhouts ;—is a fcene, in the view of
which we are almoft tempted to fay, where
were the fhields of angels ? Where the eye
of Providence ? Where the remembrance of
thofe numberlefs prayers, which had been
offered to God for the prefervation of fuch
a man, at fuch a time as this ? But let faith
affure us, that he was never more dear and
precious in the eye of his divine leader, than
in thefe dreadful moments, when if fenfe
were to judge, he might feem moft negleCted. That is of all others the happieft death,
which may moft fenfibly approve our fidelity to God, and our zeal for his glory. To
ftand fingly in the combat with the fierceft
enemies, in the caufe of religion and liberty,
when the whole regiment he commanded
fled ; to throw himfelf with fo noble an ar-
dor

dor to defend thofe on foot, whom the whole body which he headed were appointed to fupport, when he faw that the fall of the neareft commander expofed thofe brave men to the extremity of danger ; were circum-ſtances that evidently fhewed, how much he held honor and duty dearer than life. He could not but be confcious of the diftin-guifhed profeffion he had made, under a re-ligious character ; he could not but be fen-fible, how much our army, in circumftances like thefe, needs all that the moft generous examples can do, to animate its officers and its foldiers : And therefore he feems delibe-rately to have judged, that altho' when his men would hear no voice but that of their fears, he might have retreated without infa-my, it was better he fhould die in fo glorious a caufe, than have it thought that his regard to religion and liberty was but a mere pro-feffion, that was not ftrong enough to make him faithful unto death. He had long felt the force of it ; and had too high a value for his king and country, to think of deferting the truft committed to him ; too great a love for the proteftant religion, to think of exchanging it for the errors of Popery ; and rather than give way to a rebellious crew, by whofe fuccefs an inlet would be opened to the cruel ravages of arbitrary power, and

to

to the bloody and relentlefs rage of Popifh
fuperftition, he loved not his life unto the
death.*   And in this view his death was
martyrdom, and has, I doubt not, received
the applaufes and rewards of it : For what
is martyrdom, but voluntarily to meet death,
for the honour of God, and the teftimony
of a good confcience ? And if it be indeed
true, as it is reported on very confiderable
authority, that before he expired he had an
interview with the leader of the oppofite
party, and declared in his prefence " the full
" affurance he had of an immortal crown,
" which he was going to receive," it is a circumftance worthy of being had in everlafting remembrance : As in that cafe, providence may feem wonderfully to have united
two feemingly inconfiftent circumftances, in
the manner of his dying ; the alternative of
either of which he has fpoken of in my
hearing, as what with humble fubmiffion to
the great Lord of life, he could moft earneftly wifh : " That if he were not called
" directly to die for the truth," which he
rightly judged the moft glorious and happy
lot of mortality, " he might either fall in the
" field of battle, fighting in defence of the
" religion and liberties of his country ; or
" might have an opportunity of expreffing
                                          " his

* Rev. xii. 11.

" his hopes and joys, as a Chriftian, to the
" honour of his Lord, and the edification of
" thofe about him, in his departing mo-
" ments ; and fo might go off this earthly
" ftage," as in the letter that relates his
death, it is exprefsly faid that he did, " tri-
" umphing in the affurance of a bleffed im-
" mortality."

How difficult it muft be in our prefent
circumftances, to gain certain and exact information, you will eafily perceive : But
enough is known, and more than enough,
to fhew how juftly the high confolations of
that glorious fubject which we have been
contemplating, may be applied to the prefent folemn occafion. From what is certain
with relation to him, we may prefume to
fay, that after he had adorned the gofpel by
fo honourable a life, in fuch a confpicuous
ftation, God feems to have condefcended, as
with his own hand, to raife him an illuftrious theatre, on which he might die a ven-
erable and amiable fpectacle to the world,
and to angels, and to men ;* ballancing to
his native land by fuch an exit, the lofs of
what future fervices it could have expected,
from a conftitution fo much broken as his
was, by the fatigues of his campaign in
Flanders,

* 1 Cor. iv. 9.

Flanders, where he contracted an illness, from which he never recovered.

On the whole therefore, whatever cause we have, (as indeed we have great cause) to fympathize with his wounded family, and with his wounded country ; and how decent foever it may be, like David, to take up our lamentation over the mighty fallen, and the brighteft weapons of our war perifhed ;* (and Oh, how naturally might fome of us adopt the preceding words too !) Yet after all, let us endeavour to fummon up a fpirit, like that with which he bore the lofs of friends, eminent for their goodnefs and ufefulnefs. And while we glorify God in him,† as on fo many acoounts we have reafon to do, let us be animated by fuch an example to a refolution of continuing like him, ftedfaft in our duty, amidft defertion and danger, and all the terrors that can befet us around. As he, having been fo eminently faithful unto death, has undoubtedly received a crown of life, which fhines with diftinguifhed luftre, among

* 2 Sam. i. 27.
† Gal. i. 24.

X

mong thofe who are come out of much tribulation ;* let us be courageous followers of him, and of all the glorious company of thofe, who through faith and -patience inherit the promifes.† Then may we be able to enter into the comfort and fpirit of them all, and of this promife in particular; and fhall not be difcouraged, though we are called to endure a great fight of afflictions,‡ or even to facrifice our lives, like him, in defence of our religion and liberties : Since in this caufe we know, if we fhould fall like him, even to die is gain ;¶ and while his memory is bleffed,** and his name had in honor, we are affured upon the beft authority, that having fought the good fight with fo heroick a fortitude, and finifhed his courfe with fo fteady a tenor, and kept the faith with fo unfhaken a refolution, there is laid up for him a crown of brighter glory than he has yet received, which the Lord the righteous Judge will give unto him in that great expected day ; and not unto him only, but unto all them that love his appearance. 2 Tim. iv. 7, 8. Amen!

* Rev. vii. 14.   ¶ Phil. i. 21.
† Heb. vi. 12.   ** Prov. x. 7.
‡ Heb. x. 32.

H· Y M N.

Sung after the Sermon.

I.

HARK ! 'tis our Heav'nly Leader's voice
  From his triumphant feat :
Midft all the war's tumultuous noife,
 How pow'rful, and how fweet !

II.

" Fight on, my faithful band," he cries,
 " Nor fear the mortal blow :
Who firft in fuch a warfare dies,
 Shall fpeedieft victory know.

III.

I have my days of combat known,
 And in the duft was laid :
But thence I mounted to my throne,
 And glory crowns my head.

IV.

That throne, that glory, you fhall fhare ;
 My hands the crown fhall give :
And you the fparkling honours wear,
 While God himfelf fhall live."

V.

Lord, 'tis enough ! our bofoms glow
 With courage, and with love :
Thine hand fhall bear thy foldiers thro',
 And raife their heads above.

VI.

My foul, while deaths befet me round,
 Erects her ardent eyes ;
And longs, thro' fome illuftrious wound,
 To rufh and feize the prize.

www.ingramcontent.com/pod-product-compliance
Lightning Source LLC
Chambersburg PA
CBHW030809020726
47499CB00006B/1829